DOOM

Doomfire on Venus

The Solar Colonies 1

Ken Catran

Hodder
Children's
Books

a division of Hodder Headline plc

Typeset by Hewer Text Composition Services, Edinburgh
Printed and bound in Great Britain by
Cox & Wyman Ltd, Reading, Berks.

Hodder Children's Books
a division of Hodder Headline plc
338 Euston Road
London NW1 3BH

For Wendy

Contents

AD 2039

1 Journey to the Hell Planet

Yellow spurts of laser fire spat across the nose of her fighter like venom. Jily twisted in the seat, jerking the control stick back and feeling gravity press against the seat as she jerked her war plane back and up into the sheltering cloud. There were two alien craft below; she wasn't safe in the cloud, as their radar would already have her in an electronic spider-web. *Keep moving!*

She thumbed the stick, injecting more power into the thundering engines on either side of her sleek, bird-winged fighter. The big helmet pressed tightly on her head and she could hear her own breathing in the oxygen mask. She had seconds – *milliseconds* – to decide. *The aliens will be expecting me to hide, so do the opposite.* Her thoughts flashed the instruction to her hands. She shot out of the clouds and below, the criss-cross patchwork lines of Earth spread outwards. Ahead was a snub-nosed alien fighter, and even as its afterburners flared and it turned, Jily pressed the control and laser fire flashed like rocket-spears ahead. The alien fighter exploded and Jily swung round. *Don't rely on instruments – use your eyes, too.* She could hear her instructor as she craned her head in the heavy helmet, looking.

Nothing.

She was taking her Swallow round in a wide curve, tense, rigid in the seat, looking at the instruments, looking around, but nothing, nothing. The other

1

Plutonian slime-thing had vanished in clouds behind a radar-deflection screen. But it wouldn't give up – those slime-things didn't know the meaning of the word. Time to tell Control what was happening.

'Earth-Control, one destroyed, one hiding.'

The faraway crackling voice came through her headphones.

'Swallow-Four, maintain search pattern, we cannot spare support—'

Jily twisted again, the Swallow going with her body as she spun round, poisonous laser fire spitting past her. Then the fighter jarred and the engine-computer voice buzzed in her ears, 'Strike starboard engine, losing fuel, ten grams per second.' She was back in the clouds, feeling the starboard wing weaken. Get out of here! screamed the voice in her mind and she dropped out of the cloud again. The alien fighter was firing up at her. Her own laser streaks zapped towards it, but the slime-thing wasn't firing back and Jily registered with that same mind-screaming voice: not two aliens—

She cut control and the fighter dropped with a heavy, thick, jarring thud that slammed her head back against the headrest and overhead flashed something dark, heading straight for the second fighter. Oh good, very good, not two but *three*. Then her own fighter shook to an explosion. The two aliens had collided, the jaws of their trap slamming shut on themselves instead of Jily and the Swallow. Bits of fighter and scraps of Plutonian slime-thing spread themselves in a dark exploding cloud overhead; just a moment to feel the thrill of victory before she reported to Control—

'Jily.'

That wasn't Control's voice. Jily shut it out, flying her Swallow through the blue-black clouds above Earth. Her sector was clear. She had defended the Earth against the aliens.

'Jily.' Kana's voice was apologetic but firm.

All right Kana, I'm coming, she thought and flicked all her consoles into landing mode; the starboard engine cut first and she would land on the port. She felt the Swallow lock on to a homing beacon and wriggled herself more comfortably in the narrow cockpit and padded seat. Sunlight dazzled through the canopy and Jily sighed as she brought up one arm; this was always the moment she hated. With the other hand she pressed the sleeve-remote and the button clicked; she hated that little sound, too, because it clicked her back to reality. The virtual reality dream-cap rose from her face with a faint humming sound and Jily rubbed her eyes; there was Kana sitting on the end of the bed.

'Time to go,' said Kana.

Time to go. This was the most important day of her life: three days after Jily Tennoto became a JOK – Junior Operative K-class – and thirty days from when the number code would appear on her hand. Jily didn't know about the number code, only that this was the day she began senior training at Spoke, the midway space station between Earth and the Moon. Or that in five days she would see a real alien spaceship, not a make-believe computer graphic in a virtual reality helmet.

'Planet Earth against the Plutonians?' Kana saw the dream-clip label as Jily unslotted it from the helmet. 'Why make Pluto the enemy? It's too cold for anything to live there.'

'Yes, and Venus is too hot. Why anywhere?' Jily tried not to snap, but Kana's calm and practical logic always punctured her dreams. 'Training and skills are what's important and anyway, Earth will have to build fighters again if the Betels—' she broke off, hating to talk about Betels just before the Spoke flight.

'Corp says,' Kana was reciting, 'Betels are a silly rumour—'

'I know what Corp says!' Jily snapped again, without meaning to. Since her parents had been killed in that crash, Kana and Dar had been her guardians and all the family she had.

'Corp instructions say only one dream-clip per person.' Kana was pretending not to notice how Jily spoke. 'Are you taking this?'

Jily was ashamed of herself. She liked Kana, even Dar, and should have spent her last morning with them instead of under a virtual reality dream-cap, fighting hologram aliens over a hologram Earth battlefield. Especially because she was a girl of Moonbase Copernicus and Earth was just a planet overhead.

'No. White Pulsar.' Jily was admitting a corner of her private dreamworld to Kana as an apology and the older woman understood.

'Good.' She rubbed her big nose and smiled as she got up to go. 'On Earth, you can ride real horses.' The door closed.

If I get to Earth, thought Jily. The spoke-wheeled space station was only a midway point to Earth, and if she didn't keep her grades up then Corp would shunt her back to Moonbase, or even a rough mining colony on Mars. Martian colonists were genetically tinted blue, green or red for some health reason she didn't understand, and a brown-skinned girl would stick out like a sore thumb. But *Earth* would mean real air, real gravity, a *real* animal to ride – and no more sleep-cubicles so narrow that when she got up she always knocked her knees against the mirror-wall opposite.

As always, Jily inspected herself in the mirror-wall. Today, of course, she had on the high-necked blue tunic and slacks of a JOK and yes, she was good-looking, never mind what Andi said about her freckles. Or Andi's long hoot of laughter when he saw that Jily had cut her black hair short – but Andi was in for a scolding anyway, because he'd already been at Spoke a month and not even a post-spark. But communications were always glitching these days. That was supposed to be the Betel aliens – stop thinking about Betels, Jily shouted angrily at herself! Then she went through to the living area where Kana and Dar waited.

'You'll do very well, Jily.'

Dar's solemn utterance was spoiled by his glance sideways. He was short, bald and self-important, his track suit zipped tightly over a round tummy; and just waiting for me to go so he can watch tennis under his dream-cap, thought Jily. But she shook his hand and slung her tightly packed silver-grey bag over her shoulder. All her life was packed in there.

'I'll walk you to the tube.' Kana was strapping on her metal-soled overshoes.

Neither of them spoke on the short journey. Jily, because there was a strangeness about walking for the last time (she hoped) down this corridor set with hologram scenes of Earth's plant and animal life

5

which she had never seen. Below their feet, the base vibrated with life. The afternoon mine shift would be hard at work in their screw-nosed tunnellers – Jily's job if she hadn't passed her JOK grades.

'Level Two, Stop Eight,' said Kana into the tube lock screen and it blinked back green. They could already hear the rumbling approach of a tube. Kana pressed a bag of sweets into Jily's hand and spoke quickly. 'Remember that Betels are a silly rumour. Corp should know.'

'I'm not worried, Kana.' The tubes rumbling went clickety-click beside Jily.

'Send me a post-spark from Spoke.' They hugged quickly, self-consciously, as the door slid open. It shut on Kana's farewell wave and Jily sat down as the tube-train rocked very slightly into full speed. There was only one other passenger in the carriage, a woman miner, her grey tunic stained with red dust, nodding into sleep. This was the first time Jily had used the long-distance track; they were speeding under the cratered grey surface of the Moon and she was on her way to Spoke.

Kana's right – Betels don't exist, said Jily firmly to herself as the tube tracks clickety-clicked underneath; they're as unreal as my Planet Earth against the Plutonians dream-clip. She was going to Spoke; *that* was real and so was meeting Andi again and the start of flight training. Earth, too, if she worked hard enough. Jily's mind buzzed, then gave that splitting click. Opposite her, the tube screen flicked and scrambled and Jily groaned – she was supposed to be *over* this! Then, inside her brain, the splitting click zipped itself back up again and the digital readout flashed today's date: 12 March 2039.

Too important to tell Corp she'd had another attack of mindspread, thought Jily, and anyway a lot of other kids had it, too. Mindspread only affected minor communication circuits and Corp said it was harmless. Just a nerve-trauma for this first generation of moon-children, thought Jily – it won't stop me getting to Earth! Jily looked at the sleeping miner in the other seat. There was nobody else around, so Corp wouldn't find out.

The tube rails clickety-clicked underneath then stopped. The door opened. A precise zap-zap machine voice said 'Terminal Six,' *her* stop, and Jily slung her bag out of the door, skipping through after it. The door hissed shut behind her. Jily's feet skidded on the metal floor and she sat down hard to a titter of laughter.

'Your landings need practice, flight trainee,' said an unkind voice.

There were two other children in the oval, grey waiting area – a boy, brown-haired and brown-skinned, in the tan slack suit of a communications trainee, and a girl, red-haired and snub-nosed, dressed in the light green of a botany student. It was the girl who had laughed. Jily ignored her and scrambled to her feet as a harsh voice echoed loudly around them.

'JOKs, into the shuttle.'

'JOKs!' whispered the girl in disgust, but she headed down the long corridor without a backward glance. Jily and the boy followed without looking at each other; through solid airlock doors and straight into a main cargo hold, with metal containers clipped between closed round portholes.

'Cabin unit ahead, names on seats, sit down and

7

strap in.' And shut up, said the harsh tones as the airlock doors sealed with a heavy click-thud behind them.

The cabin area was through the hold. Jily stuck her bag in a locker and strapped herself into the deep, comfortable chair, looking up at the dream-cap overhead. That would make the journey pass more quickly. A little tremor ran through the spaceship. The engines are warming up already, she thought. They're not wasting any time, so we'll be in deep space soon—

'Are you scared of meeting Betels?' It was the red-haired girl again, just as unkind. 'He is.' She indicated the silent boy beside her.

She's scared of Betels, too, and trying to take it out on us, Jily said to herself. She pushed out her lips and put one finger in the air. The girl's unkind smile went, and a tall woman appeared in the cabin doorway.

She had on the black, one-piece uniform of a shuttle pilot; her face was square and hard but somehow crooked as though one side had slipped a little. One eye went down at the eyelid and the corner of her mouth was down-turned.

'Tennoto Jily, Beafor Veka, Osip—' She stopped abruptly and looked at the boy. Jily knew that voice, the same that had echoed harshly through the intercom to summon them on board. 'Are you from Earth?'

'Yes,' said Osip. Jily and Veka both gave him curious looks – an Earth-boy? 'The other boy went sick—'

'All right,' the woman interrupted. One cheek was splashed with the light yellow of a proton burn, her black hair cut short on that side and coiled into a thick plait on the other. 'Don't use your dream-caps until I say so.' She made to go. 'Taking off now, so sit back and enjoy the ride, JOKs.'

'Junior Operative K-class, if you don't mind,' said Veka with dignity.

'JOKs,' said the woman. The name Nel was yellow-lettered on her pocket. 'And forget all that rubbish about Betels.' The door slid shut again.

Jily gasped as a screen above the cabin porthole flickered into life. Standing out in hologramic detail was a huge curved chamber and in the centre a long snub-nosed shuttle, inclined on a steel ramp. There was a metal tube connecting to the side and it was beginning to withdraw. We came into the ship through that tube, thought Jily. Now a section of the curved overhead roof was sliding back and the sharp, pale dazzle of moon-glow came through.

'Ready,' came Nel's loud voice.

The cubicle jarred and there was a sudden heavy pressure on Jily's body. She could feel movement speeding up around her and glimpsed the moon's grey-cratered surface. A Gobbler was crawling over it like a giant iron beetle, cutting its own deep, straight road behind it. Then a curvature line slid past and black space sealed over the porthole. Jily knew the C-class shuttles went over a hundred thousand kilometres an hour with their proton-coil drive. Not half as fast as the Betels, thought Jily, then was angry with herself. *That* was just rumour too; Betel aliens didn't exist.

Now there was black space all around and the screen showed their take-off point to the Moon, the graphic line of their shuttle levelling out as they sped away. Green lights flashed overhead and Nel's voice came again. 'On flight path, unstrap and remember weight-lack.'

The warning was too late for Veka. She had kicked off her metal shoes, as they all had when sitting down, and unstrapped for another look through the porthole. She suddenly rose gently in the air and her cry of annoyance was worth all of Jily's fears. She laughed as Veka stopped at the ceiling and bumped a little.

'Pull me down!' she yelled.

Jily thought she saw a little smile on Osip's face for the first time. They each reached up and grabbed a foot, pulling her down. Veka sank back into her chair, red-faced and scowling. She saw Osip's smile and scowled again.

'How come you're going to Spoke, Earthkid?' She strapped herself in. 'Only Moonbase Juniors go there.'

Osip didn't answer for a moment. He was looking up at the flight co-ordinates on the cabin monitor, then through the porthole. The blackness was now lit with a cutting golden edge – the sun. 'The Sun's wrong,' he said.

'What?' snapped Veka, still red-faced and slouching in her chair.

'If we're going to Spoke, it should be bearing—'

'No.'

Her loud harsh voice echoed again. Nel is listening on the intercom, thought Jily. She must have been waiting to speak neatly on cue.

'There's been a change of plan.'

'Not Mars on this course, either!' Osip's voice rose to a high note. 'Where are we going?'

'Venus.'

That single flat word sealed the cabin in utter silence. Jily's first thought was that she wouldn't be seeing Andi this trip after all; the second was the Moonbase nickname for Venus.

The Hell Planet.

'I learned about the course change just before take-off. Three months' stay, then an Earth posting after Spoke. Corp says you will be fully briefed on arrival.'

Now Jily was trying to remember everything she knew about Venus. Most planets were cold and airless but Venus, closer to the Sun than Earth, was a furnace where even the stones melted. Acid clouds and an atmosphere split with fire-storms. The stones that didn't melt were crushed by impossible gravity.

'You know the score.' Nel's voice sounded in the utter silence. 'Corp commands, we obey. The posting came up, you were in line, you had the grades. Consider it a compliment.' Perhaps it was only the cabin intercom that made the words sound mocking. Then it clicked shut and Jily sat there, feeling 'bounced'. Once in her Plutonians dream-clip, Jily had been ambushed and shot down. Her dream-cap had given a sudden unpleasant little jerk to say she was electronically dead – bounced. She was scared, feeling bounced in her stomach. Opposite, Veka was scowling and trying to look brash, but she hitched her hands in her belt too bravely. Osip sat looking straight ahead, hands tight on his knees, his face set and closed. They felt bounced too, but Nel was right, they were Corp's kids and they knew the score. Corp decided where Junior Operatives were posted and that meant no Spoke or Andi because she was going to Venus.

The Hell Planet where not even devils could live.

2 Aliens outside

It was always wonderful swinging herself on to White Pulsar's back to settle in the brown leather saddle and gently canter the horse forward. Jily was a Moonbase girl, so yellow sun and birds squawking through a blue sky always had magic. She loved this dream-clip. When she was very young, just after the accident that killed her parents, Jily had nightmares about numbers appearing all over her body. Then Kana bought her this dream-clip and ever since she had ridden White Pulsar over the endless green fields of virtual reality.

Andi's favourite dream-clip was old Earth stock-car racing, but Jily couldn't relax getting smashed up all over the track. So she rode, imagining what real horses and real fields were like on Earth. They were only twenty-four hours into the Venus trip and her dream-clip was the only way out of boredom, tasteless food and twelve hours between thirty-second showers. An Earth-posting meant her dreams would one day come true and— The scene blanked in a lost humming moment as her helmet raised. Veka took her hand from the control with that unkind grin of hers.

'The Commander wants to see you.'

Nel had left them to settle in the first day, to get used to the thought of Venus. 'Thank you, Veka,' she said politely, pushing out her lips again and slipping on her metal overshoes. Osip was sitting back in his

13

chair, dream-cap lowered. Jily had already seen his clip, a Hard Blues music festival. And she'd sneaked a look at Veka's, a history set, Cleopatra, Queen Elizabeth I and Catherine of Russia!

It was hard to imagine the quiet Osip as part of a howling music band, and too easy to imagine Veka as a famous female tyrant.

In the cargo hold, the portholes made round circles of black space and bright stars. There was another monitor screen here showing their flight path dotting itself further and further from Moon. Twenty-four hours and two million kilometres already, Jily thought – but distances were just numbers in space. The harsh intercom voice made her jump.

'Come on through.'

The flight-deck door slid open. This was Jily's first look inside a real flight-deck and it *should* have been exciting. But for some reason that little stomach-bounce was back as she clanged through.

Jily knew the layout, of course, from virtual reality. The two pilot chairs, one set back and higher than the other. Those consoles that looked so easy to use and the heavy black control stick, studded with circuits. What she didn't expect was a motionless, brass-coloured, metal figure. A metal-glass visor covered the 'face' and the helmet-head was raised in a low crest.

'A Sixer.' Nel had seen her look. 'Moonbase kids know all about Copies, don't they?' She was in the second chair, black-booted legs propped on a console. 'It runs the ship for me.'

All the androids on Moonbase were Threes and Fours; Sixers were the latest model, and they could drive a Gobbler or even fly a shuttle. These were *very* advanced.

'Don't you have a human back-up?'

'Why?' Nel was eating chocolate. She flicked a piece over and it tumbled slowly in the lack of gravity. 'Copies don't sleep and don't answer back.' She crook-smiled and her cheek-splash glistened yellow. 'How do you feel about Venus?'

'Corp says, Corp does.'

Nel gave her a mocking look and rubbed a hand over her black, plaited coil of hair, waiting for Jily to speak again.

'What is this Venus base?'

'JOK, I'm just the shuttle pilot.'

A very senior shuttle pilot, thought Jily – the tiny gold lines on Nel's black collar said so. There was something strange and shut-off about this woman. In the pale ship lighting, that yellow splash on her cheek glistened again.

'Engine flashback on the Jupiter shuttle,' said Nel, as though her olive-green eyes had scanned Jily's mind.

'Have you been as far as Jupiter?' Silly question, Jily knew, but the only thing she could think of.

'I've been to Pluto, kid.' Nel put another piece of chocolate in her mouth. 'Back in the days when solar flare radiation could cook you, when it was a two-year hike with no dream-caps to hide under.'

'That's what I want to do!' Jily knew her face was spread in a big foolish grin of excitement, but she didn't care. 'What was it like, seeing Pluto?' The last planet of the solar system!

'Just a lump of cold, dark rock.' Nel nearly crook-smiled again, but then her strong mouth set in a rat-trap line. 'Like Venus is a lump of hot rock.' She

15

leaned back, closing her eyes. 'JOK, I just wanted to make sure you were settled in.' So, end of interview, you can leave now, JOK, said the gesture.

Jily lingered, though, as it was exciting standing on a real flight-deck for the first time. 'Can I come back—' she stopped, wincing as her mind zipped open with that splitting little crack. Mindspread! Ahead, the Pilot-Copy twitched a brass finger and beside her, Nel came alert very quickly.

'Flight control to commander!' she rapped out. Her console glowed and the Copy went motionless. 'Hellfire sideways,' she muttered as a tiny static line of interference flickered on her console screens.

'It's not serious, Commander.' Jily felt that little stomach-bounce again as Nel turned a grim face towards her.

'And just *how* do you know that?' The yellow cheek-splash glistened again.

'Mindspread, I think—'

'Mindspread! Nel slapped a black-gloved hand on the console. 'They gave me a JOK with Mindspread!'

'Most kids on Copernicus have it,' said Jily desperately. 'It's just static—'

Nel interrupted harshly. 'I don't like static on my consoles – get out.'

'I'm sorry,' said Jily unhappily.

'Out.'

Jily clanged out in her metal overshoes and stood in the cargo hold. Mindspread wasn't her fault – it happened to kids on Copernicus and everybody knew about it. It was harmless and even the other Moonbases had stopped making jokes. A tear ran down one cheek and she shut her eyes tight in frustration. Then she felt another strong ripping sensation in her mind and this time it was rage. Jily turned around and stormed back on to the flight-deck.

'You should know about Mindspread!' she shouted.

Nel's black-gloved finger was about to press a console button. She looked up and her mouth set in a grim, crooked line. 'I said, *out.*'

'There's a screening programme, all the Moonbase shuttles have it – so where've you been?'

Nel stood up, very grim now, tall and menacing. Jily didn't care. She went on, her mind wanting to split again. 'When I'm flying shuttles to Pluto, I won't be making stupid mistakes like that!'

Nel's black-gloved hand was making a fist and Jily flinched but stood her ground. The olive-green eyes bored like laser drills, then Nel sat down again. She finished at the programme and a zap-zap computer voice spoke.

'Screening programme in place.'

'Control back to Pilot-Copy.'

'Copy,' said the Copy. Obedience has a one-word vocabulary.

Nel looked out of the long forward window for a moment. 'You want to fly to Pluto? Kid, you'll spend ten years shuttling beancake to Mars and trying to make those miners pay on delivery.' She rubbed a hand over her yellow cheek-splash and Jily realised this was as close as Nel would come to saying, yes, my fault.

'I'll decide that,' she said.

'Hell fire sideways you will,' said Nel. That little mocking note was back in her voice. 'Corp will. Corp always does.' The black-gloved hand clenched a moment.

'Hell fire sideways?' queried Jily curiously.

Nel grinned. 'Uranus is practically sideways, remember? Well, I nearby got caught in its gravity field once. And getting out was just that.' Nel closed her eyes as though lost in memories, but her black-gloved hand unclenched.

'I'll go now,' said Jily.

'Suit yourself.' Nel's voice was absent, her fist still clenched as though her thoughts were further away than Venus. Jily made to go, then looked out through the forward window. Ahead, one of the shining stars seemed to be moving a little.

'Is that star moving?'

'Tel-spark; Corp laid a line to Venus.' Nel sighed but her hand unclenched. 'Control, patch centre section ahead on to the monitor.'

'Copy,' said the Copy.

'I don't really want to see it,' said Jily, but felt pleased Nel was going to the trouble. A star pattern splashed on the vision monitor like black paint set with tiny diamonds.

The moving star was closer.

'Full close-up, centre screen moving object.' There was a strange flat tone to Nel's voice.

The 'centre screen moving object' was thick and round-bodied with two big, faceted insect eyes, heavy side-exhausts and a sharp sting-tail between them. Suddenly Nel gave Jily a hard shove.

'Back to the cabin, JOK. Move!'

Jily began clanging back and the flight-deck door shut behind her; she was across the hold when a terse voice came on the intercom.

'Strap in and disconnect all non-essential equipment.'

The shuttle seemed to vibrate as though they were suddenly moving very fast and turning tightly sideways; it was impossible to tell in outer space. Veka and Osip were sitting upright.

'What's happening?' snapped the girl.

'There's – there's a strange spaceship ahead.'

'Strange—' Osip mouthed the word, Betel.

Jily sat there without speaking. She wanted to pull her dream-cap down and lose herself in electronic reality. She wanted to do anything but sit in this metal shell because she knew all the spaceship types – and that thing wasn't one of them.

'I bet you got spooked on a meteor!' Veka's loud, rude voice shook a little, though. She was thinking about Betels, too.

Betels. Jily made her lips smile tightly at Osip. Think, she said to herself – what do we know about them? Nobody on Moonbase knew anything except for rumours. Betels appeared in the solar system last year. A small, fast link-shuttle went to intercept and was left behind like it was standing still. Then, whispered the rumour, the Betels had appeared again and this time, two link-shuttles went to intercept.

And, said the rumour, neither returned.

We've sent probes into the star system, thought Jily, so maybe the stars are reaching us. Maybe something alien is sussing us out. We don't really know they're from Betelguese, which was twenty million light-years away but also, said rumour, that was just the direct course setting from their first appearance in the solar system. Dar's mates at the gym had relayed all this and Kana was a Gobbler driver – they heard everything.

Then two more link-shuttles hadn't returned, communications with Mars became patchy and another rumour said the new base on Jupiter's moon, Callisto, had been shut down.

The shuttle jarred and vibrated as though something had hit it – or scanned our systems, Jily yelled silently as she was thrown hard against the seat-straps. Veka tensed and Osip sat with that closed look, his hands tightly knotted. Jily tried to make her lips keep smiling but she knew they were twisting. Another shake-thump vibrated the shuttle and the lights flickered. The intercom clicked.

'Systems readjustment, sit tight.'

Nel's cold voice sounded like she was talking to the cargo. Jily felt a tight bouncing panic in her stomach as the shuttle vibrated again as though at top speed. Osip pressed back into his seat. She could hear her own breath now, through parted lips. The shuttle must be a full energy boost and they had to sit there, *sit there* and let the long minutes pass like tombstones. Then suddenly the door hissed open, loud as a snake, and Nel was there.

'Everyone OK?' The hard olive-green eyes flickered over them all. 'Systems shakedown, everything under control.'

'What about the alien spaceship?' demanded Veka.

'A tel-spark out of place,' said Nel flatly.

'That's not true, I saw something!' cried Jily.

'You're a JOK.' Nel's cold expression did not change. 'You wouldn't know a Betel from your belly button.' She made to leave and gave that little crooked smile again. 'Hope you didn't scare the others.' The door hissed shut.

Jily sat there, her cheeks burning like the heat of Venus was on them. She felt silly, stupid. How long would it take Veka to say something? One, two, three—

'Who graded you Operative? I hope we're not working together.'

'I saw a spaceship coming towards us.' Jily knew her voice was shaking and saw contempt in Veka's eyes. She couldn't look at Osip, either; she was hot, flushed and embarrassed. Nel wouldn't throw the shuttle around like that to avoid a tel-spark – Jily was a pilot trainee, and she knew that! Osip's silence was worse than Veka's scorn. Jily pulled her bag out from under the seat, opened it and took out her dream-clip.

'Don't fall off the horse, pilot trainee.'

Veka was really enjoying herself, but Jily didn't bite back. There would be time enough later to settle with Veka. She slotted the clip into the overhead dream-cap and pulled the helmet down. Something buzzed sharply as she clicked the seat-remote and everything sprang into life.

Something was wrong. She wasn't riding a horse over the wide open holographic spaces; she was sitting in a chair and ahead was another chair and a curved window framing black space. A big, black-clad woman stood there, beside a brass-skinned Copy. The woman's back was turned but that head was unmistakable and Jily knew at once what had happened.

The dream-cap wavelength functioned on the ship waveband and somehow the two had become linked. Maybe the power surge had done it, but when Nel left her seat with the control-cap still on, it was like looking through her helmet. Jily felt scared and naked, as though standing in the cabin itself.

Her hand went to the switch, but she stopped as Nel's voice sounded plainly. She was leaning over, speaking into a communication circuit.

'Earth–Control, it was a Betel sighting, repeat a Betel sighting. It came close enough to scan us, then disappeared.'

A tiny metallic voice was replying, too low for Jily to hear. She listened, transfixed. Nel made an impatient movement and spoke again.

'One of the JOKs saw it; the Moonbase was buzzing with rumours. We—' she broke off as the tinny voice sounded longer, then gave a strange little laugh. 'OK Earthbase, I'll make sure—'

Jily was turning up her audio to hear what Earth–Control was saying, but Nel broke off suddenly, stiffening. Jily realised with a thrill of panic what she had done. When the dream-caps were left open, they let out a very high humming noise like those little insects that used to live on Earth – mosquitoes. She had turned up the audio so the sound was higher. And Nel had heard; she was turning, those olive-green eyes about to glare directly – Jily switched off and blackness came over. She clicked off the control as the humming came through the shuttle. Nel was scanning all the circuits!

Jily lifted the dream-cap. Osip had his eyes shut and Veka seemed asleep, too. Maybe it was just the shock or anticlimax, but they hadn't seen what happened. Jily's hands fumbled with panic as she pushed her dream-cap up further, operated her chair control and let it back. She shut her eyes just as the door slid open. Then, like an extra scanning wavelength, she sensed those hard olive-green eyes glaring round the cabin.

'Who was it?' came a soft, deadly voice.

Jily sat there, heart thumping. Beside her, the other two didn't move. The silence went on and on, and Nel's presence was a threatening black shadow in the room.

'Which one?'

Say nothing – pretend to be asleep like Veka and Osip. She's bluffing, unsure, Jily thought frantically to herself and tried to stop herself tensing as Nel took a clanging step forward. Jily couldn't even let her eyelashes flutter. She tried to think about Andi, Kana, Dar, but couldn't remember their faces – only Nel's black visible presence.

The door slid shut and she nearly opened her eyes. But a tiny panic-voice screamed no, *no*, because that washed, soap smell of Nel's closeness was still in the cabin, waiting to see who moved. The door slid open again and this time, the clanging footstep was outside when it shut.

Jily made herself count to a hundred, then blink, stretch and yawn before she opened her eyes. But Nel had gone and the cabin was quiet. She relaxed and realised her hands were still tightly clasped together. Had Nel noticed? Would she think someone slept like that? No, the big, grim-faced woman would have gone for her like a laser drill at a piece of rock. Jily *knew* something was wrong – and she *had* seen an alien spaceship. And Nel's laugh during that Earth-Control transmission had sounded like 'problem solved', no need to worry about the JOKS. Why?

Jily knew she was tough enough to handle normal problems, but these were dark with unknown shadows; this time she was fighting a battle outside the virtual reality of computer hologramics. She closed her eyes, but could not sleep; she could still hear Nel's laugh sounding more unpleasant each time.

What was waiting for them on Venus?

3   Down into acid-fire

'Enjoying your first look?' Nel was being sarcastic, of course. The surface of Venus was completely hidden by thick orange cloud below the slowly descending shuttle. The entry pattern was still nearly twenty kilometres above the surface. The voyage of dream-caps, tasteless food and unending boredom was over; Nel had let them through into the pilot cabin and was seated in her chair. Her control-cap was up and Jily rigidly dared not look at it – Nel was too sharp-eyed and one glance would be a complete giveaway.

Sonic waves from the shuttle were probing the surface and sending back a frightening composite picture of Venus, coming alive like computer graphics. The surface was scarred and pitted with deep valleys and giant, craggy mountains. Jily remembered the briefing-clips Nel had given them; highlands and lowlands, valleys four kilometres deep and mountains up to fourteen kilometres high. And all of it, from top to bottom, swept with the red broom of hot hurricane fire-storms.

'Atmospheric density is a thousand times greater than Earth.' Nel was repeating what they knew; density so great it would crush solid rock and the shuttle would need all its enormous energy thrust just to stay airborne. The Pilot-Copy's brass fingers moved as easily over the consoles as Kana playing her accordion, but Jily still felt uneasy. Her generation of Moonbase adults had passed on their fears about androids. Copies were no bigger than a well-grown teenager (Dar had solemnly explained that this gave human adults a psychological advantage when ordering them around), and Copies had a metal-glass visor face. There was talk of giving them real features and Jily glanced at Nel's control-cap; she couldn't imagine a Copy with a face like Nel. She grinned.

'What do you find amusing?'

Nel's hard, olive-green eyes were on her and Jily felt a tingle of panic. Did Nel see her looking at the cap? 'Nothing,' she said.

Nel came over and sat down in her chair. Now the vision screen was sonic-picturing a long continent, burned an angry red-orange and shaped like a scorpion's pincered tail.

'Aphrodite Terra, the largest continent.' Nel's green eyes flickered at Jily and the girl felt that little panic-tingle.

'Where's our base?' asked Veka.

'On Ishtar. Only the size of Earth-Australia.' More lights flashed on the control panel and Nel flicked a switch as a signal bleeped. 'We're on the base beacon, enter cloud-cover in fifteen minutes.'

'I never knew there was a base on Venus,' said Veka.

'Oh dear, did Corp forget to ask your permission?' Nel pointed at a circular depression passing across the screen. 'Resnik crater – after Judith Resnik who died when the space shuttle Challenger exploded on take-off in 1986.'

'History,' said Veka off handedly.

Jily saw Nel's hand closing into a fist and spoke hastily: 'There are two named craters. The other one is for Christy McAuliff, who was on Challenger too.'

'So?' said Veka.

'So memory's important.' Osip was watching the crater slide downscreen. 'All that crew were very brave people.'

Nel's hand relaxed. 'The cloud cover is four kilometres thick.' And all the sunlight is reflected off, thought Jily, so inside the cloud it is as cold as Corp logic and underneath, hot as hell itself. And the atmosphere was thick with fluorine and sulphur, which together made fluro-sulphuric acid. Nel was grinning unpleasantly. 'They'd better have the entry lock open, because even this bucket wouldn't last overnight on Venus.'

Under the cloud-cover, Venusian gravity was dense enough to crush rocks and wind-storms like atomic fireballs heat-blasted the rock; poisonous acid rain hissed down into active exploding volcanoes. Whoever put a base here, thought Jily, should have named this place after the gods of Hell, not the Goddess of Love.

There must be something very important on Venus.

'All right Jokkies, go and strap in, because it's a rough ride down,' said Nel.

Even Veka was quiet as they went back and strapped in. The cloud-cover was closer now and sunlight glinted dazzlingly off the thick orange mass. Jily didn't like Nel, but the thought of that solid crook-faced woman at the controls was reassuring. The sunlight dazzled thick orange again as the shuttle flew into the mass and the temperature dropped. Sunlight could not enter the cloud and it was icy outside; but below, the heat was trapped between surface and cloud, a super-greenhouse effect that turned Venus into a fiery nightmare. The orange thickness was all around them now and Nel's voice clicked on the intercom.

'Estimated arrival, fifteen minutes.'

They were going straight through orange, ice-thick clouds that were as full of acid as Earth-clouds were of rain. Then suddenly they broke clear into glowing yellow-red heat and it was like diving from a deep-freeze into a hot oven. The cabin became a steambath and splatters of acid rain misted over the porthole. The shuttle was diving nose-down into a pitted red-orange surface below. A storm was raging and cannonballs of dust punched upward. Steel would become red-hot on that surface and softer metals would melt. Suddenly the shuttle jarred and rocked with a thudding shake and they were thrown against their straps. They heard Nel shout on the intercom.

'Venusbase: rock from a volcano, losing trim!'

She must have forgotten the intercom was still on as the shuttle twisted round and shuddered again. Then the close heavy grip of Venus's gravity caught and pulled it down; ahead now a deep valley opened like a huge red mouth before them. The shuttle was flying very close to the surface and dipping. Nel's voice came again, flat and tense, talking to the base. 'Correcting flight, estimate five minutes.' A pause, then louder. 'I'm not talking to a damned Copy. Put the base controller on!'

The vision screen flickered and they were looking through the shuttle's eyes; ahead was a circular dome, scarcely above the surface. It seemed covered with a dark purple stuff. Nel spoke again, her voice sharper.

'Purple Zero – open the lock!'

Purple Zero – the name of the base? Why wasn't

it opening! Opposite Jily, Osip and Veka were sitting tight, determined not to show any fear. Veka opened her mouth, forcing the words out.

'Hot, isn't it?'

You can't be cool in all this heat, thought Jily, and nearly giggled; Veka was too tense to fool anyone. Osip said nothing, and shut his eyes tight as Nel's voice came again sharper.

'Open, Purple Zero – I've only got time for one pass!'

A wide, black crack was opening in the purple dome. Jily felt the shuttle slow down, but it was still fast as Nel took them below the valley walls, protecting them from the dust-storm but fighting the heavy pull of gravity. Then the shuttle twitched, nose up, and Jily's stomach dipped sickeningly as the thrusters boomed deafeningly around them. The shuttle was poised in midair. The storm howled overhead as they went down backwards and Jily realised Nel was risking everything on this one turn. If they missed the slot, if the gravity was too strong . . . There was a loud thudding click and, through the vision-eyes, red-swirling Venus closed into a dark slit. Then the slit itself was closing against that red glare and they were running backwards on screeching metal rails down a narrow tunnel, slowing with another thunderous blast of the engines. Something shunted hard behind with a loud click-thud as though the shuttle had been kicked with a giant boot.

Overhead the slit closed and they were inside Venus.

There was silence everywhere, complete silence. Then Jily heard a soft noise like humming and words, also soft and sounding a little breathless.

With a shock she realised it was Nel's voice on the intercom, singing in a low tone, as though she didn't have a care in the world.

'*They said a job on shuttle-ride would suit a young JOK right.*' And a clack-clack sound as she beat rhythm on the consoles. '*But I've been twice round Pluto and it's one long endless night.*' She's singing to unwind, remind herself she's still alive, thought Jily. '*Every year from rock to rock and nothing ever changes.*'

Veka gave a high-pitched giggle of nervous laughter and the singing abruptly stopped as though Nel realised she had left the intercom on. Her voice came with an annoyed edge.

'JOKs unstrap and grab your kits,' she said, and the intercom went dead. Jily's body hurt and her knees felt weak. She was hot and very sticky, shaking all over. Veka was getting up, looking over to where Osip sat, his eyes still shut tight. 'Time to stop being a passenger, Earthkid,' she said.

Osip opened his eyes. Jily leaned over to undo his straps but he flicked her hand away. 'I'm all right.'

The cargo deck was strangely rigid under their feet. The base was sealed and weightless against Venus gravity and she pulled on metal-soled boots. Nel came out of the control cabin and her olive green eyes flicked over them. She punched buttons down the side of the main lock and it slid open. Behind, another parted at the same time, showing a lit metal corridor and two motionless, brass-skinned figures.

'Our welcoming committee. Copies.' Veka's disgusted whisper came over the silent tread of the two androids as they walked inside and began unclipping the cargo packs. Nel made a 'wait there' motion and strode quickly down the corridor.

The air in the passage was cool and smelled faintly acid. It was a shock to realise how cool, because Jily knew they were only half a kilometre below the raging intensity of atomic-scale fire-storms. Osip looked sick and took a glass of water from the cargo tank. Veka threw down her kit and leaned against the lock with a sulky sigh. Jily smiled. Veka would find it very hard to be super-cool on a planet where the ground temperature was 484°C.

Outside, the corridor curved round a corner. The walls were plated with a purple alloy, slapped on like icing – something super heat-resistant, dreamed up in a Corp lab on Earth, thought Jily. At the corner, a thick buttress of the purple-plastered steel curved up, because only the strongest metals would resist that crushing overhead pressure. Jily couldn't even think how many Copies and robot-machines were destroyed before the work even got below ground. The cost must have been enormous.

There must be something on Venus that Corp badly wants.

The cup slipped from Osip's hand and water spilled over the floor. Veka made a scoffing little noise, but Jily ignored her. It had been a rough landing, but they happened sometimes and Osip would have to get used to it. And she was feeling uneasy because there was still no sign of anyone human; even if they'd arrived in the middle of workshift, somebody should have appeared by now. Tiny butterfly-feet were running around inside Jily's stomach, telling her there was something wrong with the silence and no humans.

31

Nel's booted feet clumped across the airlock and she paused, a strange expression in her olive green eyes. The Copies had finished unloading and were passing silently out. Veka spoke with a tightness that showed her tension.

'Can we get off now?'

'Oh, please do.'

The same underlaid mockery was in Nel's voice as she stood aside. Osip and Veka went out and Jily made to follow. A tight hand grabbed her arm as Nel stepped quickly in front.

'It was you that linked my control-cap – I know!' Her big hand squeezed even tighter. 'Just keep your mouth shut about Betels, understand – shut!' She was whispering, her mouth in a tight, rat-trap, crooked line; Veka turned curiously and Jily felt the empathetic sting of Nel's words. This was between *them*.

'That was an incredible landing,' she said.

'Glad you enjoyed it.'

Nel had seen Veka and let go of Jily's arm. The olive-green shutters came back down. 'Base reception at the end of the passage.' The flat note was back in Nel's voice. 'They're expecting you.' She looked at them all and her hand went to the lock control. 'Enjoy your few hours on Venus.' The shuttle door slid shut and a moment later a purple steel lock closed in the wall.

'A few hours – what did she mean?' said Veka, puzzled.

'The orbit of Venus is much slower than Earth,' said Osip. It was the first time he had spoken since they landed. 'A Venus "day" lasts about two hundred and forty Earth days, so a few hours on Venus is still three months.'

There was a loud boom-boom jarring shudder and the base tunnel shook as something roared up the entry ramp again, then cut with a distant click-shut sound. Nel's shuttle was taking off; now Jily felt alone and scared and her stomach-bounce came back.

They still hadn't seen anyone.

Veka set off down the corridor with long, impatient strides. Osip and Jily followed. Round them was silence, purple-plastered walls and the distinctive flat smell of recycled air. She had to blink hard and tell herself all this was real. She'd gone from a metal room on Moonbase Three to a metal room on the shuttle, now a purple metal tunnel on Venus. It was like a drab, unending dream-trip, but dream-trips were always slightly artificial – and all this was too, too real. They were sealed in a totally artificial gravity that made their metal shoes almost too heavy. The door at the end, Nel had said. A light glowed overhead and Jily hoped Nel remembered to input their voice prints in the audio lock.

'Tennoto, Jily, JOK reporting for duty.' Osip and Veka echoed their names, the light blinked off and the door hissed open.

Inside was a large, six-sided room. A row of consoles and Copy-control caps lined one wall and their monitor screens showed another plain room that must be the mining shaft entrance. The door by the consoles would lead to that and opposite, another door was marked 'Quarters'. Where they would live and sleep. The other walls were Corp's favourite colour of plain light yellow, except for the centre one, facing the consoles – it was a glossy medium blue.

There was nobody in the room.

A faint humming sound came from the generators underfloor. Veka opened the 'Quarters' door, then ran over to the other. Through it was a platform and steps and Veka clattered down, shouting, 'Anybody there – anybody?'

Osip listened to her shout echo back from the purple-plastered walls in that closed way of his. 'Nobody down there,' he said. He'd guessed already, and so had Jily even before Veka's metal-soled boots came clattering back up the stairs.

They were alone on Purple Zero.

4   Death at the rock-face

'Hello. My name is Angharad.' The voice that spoke was warm and friendly, with a rich note of musical laughter. Jily and Osip just looked, at the voice and image that suddenly sprang into life before them. Veka appeared at the top of the stairs and walked forward, goggling with the same amazement.

The blue centre wall had disappeared as though slid aside. Through it was another room, carpeted in a soft yellow. A woman was looking at them, seated casually on the side of her desk. The top was a solid slab of crystal. She was very attractive, with shoulder-length black curls, tinted in hologramic silver. Her face was painted in the latest lines of straight make-up bands and her jacket and slacks were cut beautifully in shimmering layers of artificial silk. Behind her was a window, opening out into a lovely contrast of green parkland and blue skies. Jily guessed at once, but Veka was flushed, angry and scared.

'What the hell are you playing at?' She came storming up, past Jily over to the woman. 'Why—'

Angharad threw up a hand to stop her and her blue-painted lips framed a warning. Too late. Veka walked slam into the wall, recoiled and sat down hard.

'I should have mentioned I'm a hologram transmission from Earth.' She sounded apologetic but kept a hand over her painted lips. The fingernails were long and each was set with a small hologram flower that kept changing. 'Not hurt, I hope dear? Except perhaps in pride?'

Veka got up, rubbing her nose and shook her head, muttering something. It was a very real hologram transmission thought Jily, the best she'd ever seen. She almost felt she could walk into that room herself.

'Osip, Veka and Jily. You shouldn't be in Purple Zero on your own, but you are quite safe.' The blue-painted lips went reassuringly solemn. 'You are perhaps the most important children in the solar system. Corp needs you. And so does World Council.' She added the mention of Earth government as though it was an afterthought.

'Where is everyone?' said Osip.

Angharad looked at him. That screen must have two way visual transmission, thought Jily, an incredible piece of hi-tech for a mining base.

'There were three Junior Operative K's before you, and their Controller.' Not JOKs thought Jily – that beautiful mouth framed the full title like a set of precious stones. 'The Controller was Parthenope, a senior minerals specialist.' Parthenope, another real Earth name, thought Jily. 'We intended to double the workforce – and production.'

'What happened?' said Osip.

'There's a rockfall at the end of the tunnel below,' said Veka. Her face was white.

'They're under it,' said Angharad. She pressed blue-painted lips together in a smooth face and just for a moment, looked like someone else Jily knew. 'There was nothing we could do. It was tragic.'

The last three words were added on like 'World

Council' had been before. She doesn't look very sorry, thought Jily, just careful. Angharad's eyes flickered a little and Jily knew there was someone else, just outside the transmission frame. She could just glimpse the hint of a shadow.

'A first base was built for exploration last year by android mining-remotes. Then Purple Zero itself, and work must continue at once. The construction cost in Copies alone—' She gave a little grimace and Jily knew why. Even the new Sixer Copies wouldn't last long on the surface of Venus and it must have taken a long time to construct the dome before tunnelling could begin.

'Do we have to dig out that rockfall?' Osip's voice shook a little.

'No.' Angharad smiled with just the right touch of sympathy and that little shadow of movement edged away again. 'Parthenope was changing the Copy programme to a new direction when – when it happened.' The flower-painted fingernails came together again in a neat clasp. 'We'll give you readouts and your shuttle commander has orders to return with more personnel as soon as possible.'

'And ordered not to say we were alone,' said Jily.

'Yes. I gave those orders.' Angharad looked directly at her and Jily sensed she had seen that face before.

'What are we looking for?' Osip's question was so simple and obvious that Jily hadn't even thought about it.

'An energy source.' Angharad's eyes glowed blue. 'So powerful it will generate our entire output for –

37

for a very long time. But only one person knew where it was. Parthenope.'

Who is under the rock-face, complete with secret, thought Jily. There were a hundred questions she wanted to ask, but Angharad skipped off the table and clasped her hands, smiling again.

'So. Get some rest before you begin. Work hard and Corp will be very generous.' She looked for a moment as though she was going to step out of the hologram into the room – then one graceful finger went to a control button on the desk.

'Who's in charge?' demanded Veka suddenly.

The flower pattern flash-changed on Angharad's fingernail as she pointed. 'Beside you.' Then the screen clicked and flickered back into the blue glossy wall. Veka looked incredulously beside her and so did Jily . . . at Osip between them.

'Me?' he said.

'I'm not taking orders from *him*,' shouted Veka at the empty screen.

'We both are,' said Jily. She didn't want to either, as Veka *was* a better leader than Osip and there was something wrong with all this. Veka swung round to glare at her.

'We're equal grades!'

'Then ask Corp when the woman comes back,' said Osip in a low voice. 'We'd better get something to eat, then go to sleep.'

'Yes, I will ask Corp!' shouted Veka. 'You nearly wet your pants coming down – I saw you!'

Osip just turned and headed for the sleeping quarters. Stop, come back, face her down, thought Jily, and if she smacks you then smack her back! Veka was a booster, set to climb the Corp ladder, and Osip would have to out-boost her. He won't, though, she thought. Not his style – and not Corp's style to make a mistake like that.

The sleeping quarters were a standard Moonbase layout. There were eight bunks with waist-high partitions, each set with a shiny pointed dream-cap that glistened with new hi-tech, maybe even simulating real smell and movement, thought Jily. A table and chairs, the food machines, showers and toilets. Jily punched out hot tea and a protein bun and sat at the table. Osip sat awkwardly at the other end and Veka pointedly took her food to a bunk. Jily yelled silently at Osip again: order her to sit at the table, make us into a unit – but he wouldn't.

A hundred questions? No, she had a thousand.

Corp must have known there was nobody alive on the base. And why were they looking for something they didn't know anything about? How could that one person, Parthenope, strike such an incredible bargain with one of the Big Five? Corp owned half the moon, a quarter of Mars – but Parthenope had laid down the law. That was all just too wrong.

In fact, something was awesomely wrong.

Osip finished his meal and disappeared into the showers. Veka at once came over and sat beside Jily. She even smiled and her voice was soft. 'He'll fold up. You and I should be running this place,' she said, smiling again. Meaning you with me second in command, thought Jily. 'We'll tell Corp now, OK?'

'Corp's shut off.'

'We'll raise them again. They'll be monitoring,' said Veka. She gave another tight smile. 'That guy's useless.'

Maybe, thought Jily, but Corp chose him. And

Corp *would* be monitoring for a project this important. They would even be listening right now because this was *their* base under Venus. She wasn't taking sides until she knew a lot more, and anyway it was too good a chance to put Veka in her place. She raised her voice just a little.

'Corp's made the decision, Veka. And we have to make it work – OK?' She gave a big smile. 'Just do what Osip tells you.'

Veka hadn't missed the slight rise in her voice and instantly clicked what Jily was doing. Her blue eyes flashed like Martian rock-crystal, her smile went into a tight line and she took a deep, hissing breath. 'OK!' she muttered in a drop dead tone of voice and got up. Jily had already moved her leg and Veka's swinging foot connected with the chair instead of her ankle. Jily smiled again, her hand up in a fist. Veka just glared and went back to her bed, limping slightly, Jily was pleased to notice. There were too many kids like Veka on Moonbase and scoring off them was sweet, very sweet. She was still smiling when Osip came back into the room and walked up to her.

'I heard that.' He gave a pale smile. 'Thanks.'

He went over to his bunk. I did it to keep *my* place not yours, Jily wanted to shout, wake up kid! She felt a bit ashamed now and went to her bunk. Was this the real world of being almost grown-up – playing little power games and scoring off people? With a shock she remembered there were fire-storms raging overhead that would instantly turn them, and their jealousies, into black ash.

She put on her sleep-shirt and got into bed. The lights on either side went out, but Jily wasn't sleepy. She pulled the dream-clip down over her head. She always thought better, riding White Pulsar.

Jily recoiled as the clean wind blew into her face. These new dream-caps were good! The wide endless field was green and real and beside her, White Pulsar neighed, nuzzling her cheek with a wet nose – wet! Jily gasped – these new dream-caps were *real* and there was a wonderful new release in mounting the big white stallion and riding forward. To see bits of brown realistic earth fly up under his thudding hooves and his mane flicking her face as she bent forward! The grass was so green and the sky that lovely deep blue of Angharad's eyes. Angharad the Earth-woman.

Jily had always wanted to go to Earth. She wanted the magic of eating natural foods, getting a real suntan and swimming in seawater. And riding a real horse, not an enhanced hologram. And Earth people were always tall and good-looking, with fascinating names like Angharad, Meredid, Zephyrine or Telesforo. Or even Parthenope – and she shuddered. Having a great name didn't stop someone ending up under a rockslide. Jily reined in White Pulsar – she couldn't let herself think like that.

'Corp needs me. I'm important,' she said aloud to herself, inside the dream-cap. 'Do this right, Jily, and you'll be under the blue skies of Earth.' She felt better saying that to herself. She clicked the dream-clip off and the helmet rose from her head. Jily lay back and closed her eyes. A black space-time later, the musical tones of wake-up piped round her.

They showered and put on one-piece overalls. The garments were fresh and cool, but Jily repressed a

41

little shiver as she thought about who had worn them last.

'I'll check the Copy programmes for the new settings,' said Osip. It was still only a suggestion and Veka pretended she hadn't heard. To Jily's annoyance, Osip repeated himself. But she just finished her breakfast of egg cake and the white plastic stuff that Corp said was milk, and kept her mouth shut.

Osip hesitated, then went out; Jily counted to three and followed. Veka must have counted to twenty before she slowly got up and sauntered after them.

In the control room the blue vision screen was blank. Osip punched the calling button, but nothing happened. Even that blue glossy wall was saying, get on with it. Go down the steps and face the rock-fall that is a tomb.

Osip stopped by the control consoles and voice-activated the Copies. There were four on the base; two stood in narrow alcoves like upright coffins beside the consoles. Even their blank, visored faces looked at Osip with the same message. Get on with it, face the rock-fall and don't think about those bodies. Osip went over and opened the door. He paused again, then went inside and Jily followed. All right, you've made your first decision, she thought.

The mining chamber was much larger and looked as though it had been hollowed out with a Gobbler-scoop. A small platform ran to one side and a row of steps, cut from the rock, led down. There were two more Copies below in stone coffin-alcoves. A chain link of buckets ran across the centre to a small airlock set in the side. Rubbish vent to the surface, thought Jily. Osip paused, moving a little to one side as though asking them to go down the steps before him. Veka made to and Jily moved sideways, blocking her body. Osip began to walk down the steps. Decision Two thought Jily.

The thick, purple metal icing stopped halfway down the chamber then met the blue rock-face veined with red and gold sparkles. Jagged little splinter-lines of silver ran through it. At the end, an untidy jumble of sparkling rocks spelled the ugly face of death and over to the side, another rough semi-circle had been chiselled out in the rock-face. The air was still cool and another little half-question formed in Jily's mind as Osip pointed at the new markings.

'That must be where we start work.'

'Where the Copies start work,' said Veka. 'Catch me using a laser drill.'

Osip gave her a worried look. 'We have to work together, Veka—' then he stopped as though apologising.

'Then tell Corp I'm in charge.' Veka's eyes glinted like killing crystals. 'I'll get things moving.'

Osip's moment of decision and he couldn't handle it, Jily knew that. All right then, sink under, she thought. Then that half-question tripped off her tongue just before Osip nodded to Veka. 'Why hasn't this place heated up?'

The purple icing went only halfway and above was the terrible burning flameland of Venus. But down here, the air was cool as Moonbase – even outside the protection shield.

'Why—' Osip broke off, looking past her. So did Veka, her hazel eyes widening. Jily turned round.

The two Copies below had stepped out of their

43

stone coffin-alcoves and with inhuman quickness, grabbed laser drills from the racks.

'Copies – freeze,' commanded Osip. They kept moving, making no noise on their metal feet. 'Copies – freeze!' Osip gave Jily a push and she didn't have to be told twice. Neither did Veka. They turned for the stairs, then stopped.

The two Control-room Copies were coming down, hands at sides but metal fingers curling. They moved silently, their metal feet making no sound in the deadly hush – a hush cut by yellow flare-tongues of laser as the Copies below flicked on their drills. There was a deadly cutting hiss that spoke cold murder in the silence.

'Copies – freeze!' Osip's voice cracked with the tension, but it made no difference. All three children backed up against the stone end-wall as the Copies formed a neat line in front of them.

They were trapped.

5   Copy-murder

'Great voice-ac you've got,' yelled Veka.

'It should be working, Copies *never* do this!' Osip's voice cracked again.

Well they *are* doing it, screamed Jily to herself as the four faceless metal androids advanced in a stalking line, unspoken death in their movements. Jily felt that horrible stomach-bounce of fear. She had never liked Copies and two of them were holding laser drills that could slice her into neat cubes of protein.

Veka picked up a chunk of rock and threw it at a Copy. It bounced off the visored face and the thing didn't even hesitate. The laser drills flared and they continued their silent advance. Jily picked another rock and threw it. Veka grabbed a long metal probe and lashed out. The Copies kept coming. They were being herded up against the rock-face and there was no escape. Jily's foot kicked one of the trolleys and she looked up at the overhead chains.

'Osip, slip the chains at your end,' she whispered.

Osip was white-faced and open-mouthed. He looked up and seemed to hesitate. 'Do it!' she shouted and Osip spun the securing wheel. The chains slackened and crashed down, wrapping round the two Copies, knocking them together. They both crashed back into a third and Osip sprang forward, underneath them. A fourth turned to leap after him with a tigerish spring.

Veka leaped to follow, but her foot caught in a coil of chain and she stumbled. Jily pulled her up but the three Copies were kicking themselves free and the laser drills flared.

'Osip!' she screamed.

Osip had tripped on the stairs. Blood ran from a cut on his forehead and the fourth Copy grabbed at his leg. Osip tugged free with what seemed a wail of panic and ran up the stairs. The Copy ran after him, a metal arm outstretched.

Jily dragged Veka free. 'You coward!' the red-haired girl screamed after him, but the door slid shut, just ahead of the Copy's grasping fingers. 'You stinking yellow—' Another laser drill swung and both girls recoiled, their backs against the rock-face.

Veka was jabbing her probe ahead, her face furious. Jily picked up another rock and threw it, her stomach contracting as the laser drills pointed their yellow tips at it. There was silence upstairs; the fourth Copy had forced the door open and gone through. Osip wouldn't escape from the fast-moving creature, for there was nowhere to hide.

Now Jily was stumbling over the collapsed debris of the rock-face and kept throwing lumps of rock at the Copies. It was like pelting them with moondust. Veka lunged again with the probe, but the Copy caught it in super-quick metal fingers, wrenching it from her fingers. It reversed the probe and stabbed forward. Veka grabbed it, but the Copy was too strong. It swung her like a fish on the end of a line and threw her down against the rock-face. The second Copy was aiming a laser drill at Jily, brass finger flicking the switch to full power. Beside her the first Copy stabbed viciously down and Veka's agonising scream was cut hideously short. Jily shut her eyes and screamed with a high choking sound, like a trapped animal.

The heat flared in her face and she jerked her head sideways. The same heat burned her cheek and she sucked hot air into her mouth, opening her eyes. The Copy standing over her was rigid and the blank face glared with frustrated hate. Jily moved her face away from the still-hissing laser. Veka's Copy was standing over the girl's limp body and Jily averted her eyes as she saw the blood. Veka must have been skewered like protein on a fork.

She couldn't move. It was as though her own body was locked tight and as unmoving as the Copy standing over her. There were running feet on the stairs and Osip appeared, white-faced under his brown skin. There was a cut-off button at the back of each Copy's neck. Osip switched off each one, then knelt beside her.

'Jily!'

She was still rigid and trembling with fear. She blinked and rolled her eyes at Veka's body, then away again. The shudder of horror, the sudden need to be sick, unfroze her body and she rolled over. She coughed and heaved, her face between her knees, unable to stop shuddering. Osip was kneeling beside Veka's body, making tugging motions. He was pulling the probe from the Copy's tight-locked metal fingers.

Jily got to her knees. Her face was pale and she still wanted to be sick. Osip uncurled stiff metal fingers and the probe clanged on the floor. She heard him give a little sob as he picked up a limp hand. Jily tried to get up, but couldn't. She crawled

47

over to Osip, sharp pieces of rock cutting her knees through her overalls. Veka lay with a spreading patch of blood over her stomach. Osip looked over. 'I think the point just broke her skin.' He was pulling open the tear in Veka's suit with strong fingers. 'She's all right.' Veka gave a low moan and opened her eyes. 'She just fainted.'

'It's over Veka, over.' Jily patted her hand, she couldn't think of anything else to say. 'Over, over.' Together they pulled Veka to her feet and dragged her past the frozen metal hands and glaring blank faces.

'Take it easy,' said Jily. Veka pushed off her arm and stood, leaning white-faced against the wall, her red hair wet and straggly. A smear of blood appeared as she rubbed her face and looked back at the silent Copies. Their blank faces still looked full of menace.

'I overrode their programme on the computer,' said Osip. 'They're safe now.'

'Safe . . .?' whispered Veka. She picked up a big rock-hammer and swung it with a sudden strength. The first Copy snapped its metal head sideways and collapsed. The effort made Veka wince with pain and Jily grabbed the hammer, swinging at the second. The thwacking metal sound was very satisfying. Then the third, and it collapsed over the other two. Osip kneeled, opening each visor and wrenching out the control-circuits. Electronic brains sparked dying soul-fire under his fingers and yellow fluid smeared his hands like pale blood.

'One more upstairs,' said Osip. Veka pressed her hand over her stomach again and went up the steps ahead of them both. Jily paused.

'Osip, you saved our lives.' His pale smile became a little self-conscious grin as he followed Veka up the stairs to where the smashing sound had already started. The Copy that had run after Osip was already crumpling to the floor by the control chair. Veka's hammer swung mercilessly, her face set with hate.

'It must have got very close to you,' said Jily.

'I moved very quickly,' said Osip with another little grin.

So do Copies and that one got very close, thought Jily. She had already seen the black marks on Osip's throat under the ripped collar of his suit – marks made by steel fingers closing round his throat as he sat at the keyboard, inputting a cancellation code. That took special cold nerves and she shuddered. Veka threw down the hammer on the smashed remains of the Copy. There was some colour back in her pale cheeks.

'Do you know what they cost?' said a cold voice behind them.

They turned. The glossy blue wall had opened and Angharad stood there. Her cold expression changed as she saw the ripped suits, the scorch-mark on Jily's tunic and Veka's bloodstain.

'What happened?'

'Copies!' said Osip. He ripped off what was left of his collar and the black clutch-mark showed clearly round his neck. Jily had seen Copies crumble solid rock in their hands; another moment and Osip's neck would have snapped like a rotten stick.

'Copies have never before become deranged!' said Angharad. For a moment she looked very scared and flicked her eyes sideways to that unseen person again. She looked at Osip's neck and her composure

49

came back. There were different lines of make-up on her face and her hair was blue, tinted with hologramic green that flashed from light sea-fire to dark emeralds. Her fingernails were painted in the same changing shades of green. 'You must have moved very fast.'

'I had to,' said Osip.

'Yes, your precious androids tried to kill us!' screamed Veka. She can still feel that point on her stomach, thought Jily.

'We made a good choice of unit leader,' said Angharad. An approving smile came smoothly to the green-painted lips. She seemed to accept that Copy attack very quickly, thought Jily – or maybe it just didn't touch her, safely back on Earth.

'Yes, you did.' Jily could say that honestly. Veka pressed a hand over her stomach again but said nothing.

'All right. Deactivate the Copies and work the laser drills yourselves.' The green-painted lips set wryly. That woman always has her face under perfect control, thought Jily. 'You must carry on. We know you will succeed.'

'And what else might go wrong?' said Osip.

'There are no more Copies on the base.'

'Well, what got into those ones?' Jily had never heard herself scream like that. 'The same things that sent our shuttle systems haywire?'

'The two problems are not related.' Angharad's words were polished steel. Then her voice softened a little and the blue eyes dwelled on Jily. 'Relax.' Jily had the same little feeling of knowing Angharad from somewhere. The screen flickered into glossy blueness.

'I'm going to lie down,' said Veka abruptly. She paused, hands very formally to her sides as though embarrassed. 'Thank you.' Then she headed for the sleeping quarters.

'Yes, thanks Osip,' said Jily. He gave her a shy little grin and she found herself grinning back.

'You supported me, remember?'

'I did that to score off Veka.' What a silly time to be honest, she thought. And she could tell by the way Osip shrugged that she had hurt him. 'But I could never be brave like that, either.'

Jily was glad to see that little grin come back. She rather liked it. Together they pulled the broken Copy down into the mining chamber. It was astonishingly light and the metal heels clattered on the stairs. They pulled all the Copies apart and left them in an untidy jumble of heads, arms, legs and bodies in one corner.

'We're really on our own now,' said Osip.

Jily hadn't thought about it like that, but they were. And there was still that sense of unreality as though the fire-storms raging overhead didn't exist. Nothing existed outside the purple-plastered walls of Purple Zero and Jily felt very tired. They'd only got up an hour ago, but the aftershock was setting in. Her body ached and she kept shivering.

She went back up to the sleeping quarters. Veka was already on her bed, eyes shut and lying sideways, arms wrapped round her body. Jily punched out a cup of hot coffee and drank it. Real coffee-beans the machine label said, but she doubted it now. Everything about Corp seemed more artificial with each passing hour. She was on her bed with her eyes shut when Osip came in. Jily didn't want to talk to him or to anyone – she only wanted to lie there and ask herself all those many questions that had no answers. She felt light-headed, sick and was still shivering.

I want to be a section leader, Jily thought. I want control and security, but could I think as fast as Osip? Could I be as cold and decisive as Angharad? I was ready to panic, she thought; even Veka was braver than me. She reached up and pulled down her dream-cap, slipping the clip into it. The screen pressed against her eyelids, then sprang into a startling virtual reality life in her mind.

She galloped White Pulsar for several minutes, letting the fresh cold air blow against her face and stream through her short hair. Then she reined in, and the sky seemed bluer, the grass greener. The distant tree-line was more real and Jily felt a tingle and sense of life that she'd never experienced under a virtual reality helmet. Was the sun even burning a brighter yellow? She knew that she liked Osip; even inside the virtual reality hologram trip, her body felt a warm inside-boosting at the thought of him.

Around her everything seemed to slip out of focus for a moment. Jily reined in White Pulsar and looked around. She had a feeling that something was changing, *had* changed. White Pulsar neighed, wanting to be galloping again. Jily kept a tight hold on the reins and looked round, because a little strange feeling was in her body – and then she saw why.

There was someone else in her dream-clip.

Dream-clips were solo things unless otherwise programmed. They were a way of escaping from everything, a locked room that nobody could enter. Jily had always galloped White Pulsar over the greenlands towards the distant tree-line with birds flying overhead. In front of her someone stood beside a black horse, looking at the same tree-line.

Jily nudged White Pulsar into a canter. The other person did not turn, even though White Pulsar's hoofbeats were loud and certain. Jily reined in and dismounted. Keeping one careful hand on the reins, she went forward. She had seen that head and shoulders before and knew who it was, even before the person turned round.

'Osip.'

6   Where Hell freezes

Osip gaped and pulled hard on the reins as he took
a step backwards. The black horse whinnied and he
looked round. Then his hand went to the remote on
his sleeve.

'Don't disconnect,' Jily yelled.

She was too late. Osip had pressed the little button.
Then he pressed it again – and again, she could hear
it click in the utter stillness.

'Where did you come from?' he yelled, taking
another step back. The horse whinnied again.

'We must have the same dream-clip – we've cross-
sliced, that's all.' Even as she said it, she knew it was
stupid, impossible. But she kept walking forward, her
hand out.

Still very scared and tense, Osip put out his own
hand and their fingertips touched. 'This can't happen.' He swallowed and shook his head. 'Dream-clips
can't mix, even if there was interference—' He broke
off and shook his head. 'We couldn't touch like this
– and why doesn't my remote work?'

'I don't know,' said Jily. 'Something on Venus—'

'You.' Osip was still scared, but thinking again.
'Your dream-clip is controlling mine.' Their hands
remained touching. 'Like standing in someone else's
dream.'

'That's not technically possible,' said Jily.

'Something on Venus . . .'

'. . . Means we can talk inside a cross-spliced

dream-clip. Like telepathy and dreams mixed together.'
Jily took her hand away, thinking Osip might vanish.
He gave another uncertain headshake.

'We should tell Corp.'

'Corp! Why?'

Osip flinched at her sudden flash of temper.
'Because—'

'Because the base belongs to them? All the more
reason not to!' Jily shouted. A light breeze began
blowing round her.

'What—'

'You really are an Earthkid, aren't you?'

'So? How does that make me different?' Osip was
getting angry now; both were forgetting about their
double dream together.

Jily let go of the reins of White Pulsar and turned
her face into the breeze. She had to think about
herself to answer this, about Moonbase and being
a Junior Operative K-class.

'You were born on Earth. You know what real
grass is like, real skies, even real horses.' She ran
her hands through White Pulsar's mane. 'But Veka
and I don't. Food and water are processed, there are
no days or nights and if you want to see an animal,
you punch a hologram.'

'But you can get to Earth—'

'If we're good kids and Corp approves. Osip,
Moonbase units are small and Corp scans everything
– the only private place is under your dream-cap.'
Osip said nothing and beside them, the two horses
gently touched muzzles. 'So living a dream-clip like
this is – is magic, and I'm not going to share it
with Corp.'

Osip looked at her steadily. 'Is that your only

reason?' He waited a moment, then tried a little smile. 'If you don't mind telling an Earthkid . . .?'

'Osip, nothing's right here.' Jily tried a little smile back. 'That spaceship I saw – it wasn't a tel-spark. Nel's as tough as they come and she was scared. And the Copies attacking us – Angharad wasn't surprised when we told her. They must scan this place like Moonbase.'

'And if they'd killed us?'

'Corp would have got three more JOKs.' Jily's smile was cold. 'We're expendable.'

'Veka?'

'We can't tell her. She's a booster and she'd score points telling Corp.' The breeze was rising and Jily shivered this time.

'Maybe Angharad's not telling Corp everything – Corp always looks after its people.'

'Maybe, Osip. But there's something very wrong on Purple Zero and this –' she touched hands again '– is part of it.'

'And somewhere we can talk.' he said.

'Yes.' He understood and Jily was so relieved she wanted to fling her arms round him. She just smiled, though, and mounted her horse.

Osip did the same. 'What do you call him?'

'White Pulsar.'

'Black Solar.' He grinned. 'Not very original.' Now Jily was picking up on how more assured he was in the virtual reality world, more determined.

'Osip, why aren't you like this on—' She was going to say 'Venus', but that wasn't right because they were on Venus and living this wide, open space in their heads.

'I'm trying. But I'm letting Veka get to me. I don't know why they made me leader.'

'You were great with the Copies. Listen, Veka pushes everyone – just push back.' She put out her hand. 'This is where we do our talking – right?'

'All right.'

Osip put his hand in hers and Jily felt a nice thrill go through her body. His hand was big and warm and as strong as hers.

'I'll go now.'

'OK. Thanks, Jily.'

She had another nice feeling when he spoke her name. Then her fingers touched the remote and a click-moment later, Jily was back in her bunk with the dream-cap rising from her head.

Osip's cap was rising over the partition next to her, but she didn't call out. That would somehow destroy a nice memory. She pulled the cover up and lay back, closing her eyes. There was a lot to think about, but she fell asleep before she could start and this time, she had real dreams about Osip.

They had been less than twenty-four hours on Venus.

'Start at right angles,' said Angharad. She had on a shimmering red, long-skirted garment. Her hologramic fingernails were roses, into orchids, into lilies and her lips were painted white against the vertical contrast lines of blue. Blue-white hair fell round her blue-eyed face. 'Nel will be back in about ten Earth-days, but progress is vital.' Her white-painted lips framed that word again. 'Vital. Questions?'

'No questions, Director,' said Osip and received

another white-painted smile before the screen smoothed into a glossy blue. Veka was already heading downstairs and had a laser drill up the rock-face when they arrived. Osip hesitated and Jily nudged him.

'I'll start work with the drill,' he said, reaching out to take it. 'You and Jily work the chute.'

'Will I *please* work the chute,' snapped Veka. 'I'm not a Copy.'

'Will you and Jily *please* work the chute,' said Osip with a big level smile at her. Good one, thought Jily, nice and easy and nothing heavy; you'll make a leader yet. She nearly laughed at the scowling look on Veka's face.

The chute was an oval-shaped flap set in the wall that shot the rubbish up with compressed air and through another airtight lock on to the surface. It was airtight to stop burning poisonous gas returning with it. Even so, a slight smell of burning and sulphur came out when Jily lifted it and she remembered another question.

'This is wrong,' she said. 'We're out of the insulated area, but it's not cold. All of Venus is on fire overhead and we should feel it.'

'Well, we don't.' Veka was still sulking over losing the drill.

Osip nodded. 'Check the outlet. It might be blocked up top.'

There was a narrow side-door by the chute that opened into rough stone steps cut out of the rock. It made an unpleasant locking sound behind Jily and she was only a little way up when she felt the heat. So why was there none in the mining chamber? It grew hotter and hotter as she went up and when she reached the little walkway at the top, the heat was striking her like a solid blow. She pressed a button to open the purple heat-resistant cover and found herself looking at the surface of Venus.

'The top' was a small astrodome of iron glass – two metres thick, the briefings had said – that controlled two robotic probe arms in case the chute was blocked on the outside. The iron glass was tinted, but even so, the red glare struck at her eyes like a tiger's claws. A red and yellow fire-storm raged around, hammering down into a baked and lifeless surface. The sweat was already running down her body and heat blasted unendingly into her face. Two purple-sleeved robotic arms extended to the outlet vent, but it was clear. Jily looked round at the howling storm-blast of fire. Nel had brought her spaceship down into this and tucked them neatly into the base. She was a fantastic pilot, but Jily wished she could like her more.

As she watched, the tube opened a black eye and square chunks of rock bounced out to join a crumbling pile, already being squashed flat by the invisible pressing hand of Venus gravity. There was a big flattened pile already forming. We're making mountains of rubbish on Venus just as we did on Earth, thought Jily as she pressed the button to close the purple cover. As she did, red light glinted on letters that someone had scrawled on the inside of the iron-glass, showing clearly for a moment:

DOOMFIRE. ANDI.

Andi! The cover shut over, but the word stayed with Jily as though written inside her mind. Andi must have written it; his little flourish over the 'A' was unmistakable. So he was here before . . . then Jily remembered Andi was still here but it was too much of a shock to feel anything yet. The tears would have to come later. And now it was too stunning, even to talk about, even to open that cover and look at the scrawled word again. Those first JOKs . . .

No wonder Andi had not sent a post-spark from Spoke.

They worked all morning. Veka used the laser drill after Osip, then Jily. If Osip noticed how silent she was, he said nothing. Setting the yellow cutting flame was easy, but the drills were heavy and wrists soon ached. Jagged slabs of rock were cut out and sent up the chute to the surface. In three hours they had cut a metre into the rock-face and Jily was asking herself if she even saw that scrawled word – and if she dared even to look again.

Osip tested the rock as they went. Jily had to look away when he did that. It reminded her of the other rockfall – and Andi. 'Looks solid enough,' he said. 'Let's have lunch.'

Lunch? Jily had no idea of Moon-time. Mornings and afternoons became nothing when the lights were always on and one Moon-day was a few Venusian minutes long. 'We still don't know what we're looking for,' came Veka's voice from behind.

'We know what we've got,' said Osip. He held out a piece of rock, veined with thick yellow streaks. 'Gold, these rocks are full of it.'

'So what? Gold's not important these days,' said Veka, puzzled.

Osip looked at her. 'Do you know what makes the surface so hot?' he said. 'All the carbon dioxide

61

has been squeezed out by the enormous gravity pressure.'

Jily nodded. Yes, like juice from an orange, and it's trapped under the cloud cover, making the atmosphere very poisonous and hot. That was standard briefing stuff – then she realised what Osip was saying. A soft metal like gold should have melted.

'I'm going to run these rocks past the mineral scanner. If the gold is OK, then maybe the gas content is too.'

'That's impossible, this close to the surface,' said Veka.

'It's impossible we're not feeling more heat, even though we're outside that purple stuff,' said Jily. 'Something is keeping us cool. Very cool.'

'An underground river?' said Veka.

Osip shoot his head. 'This close to the surface? Purple Zero would be a steam bath.' Veka just shrugged, threw the rock back to him and snapped her visor shut. 'Hey, we'll take a break,' said Osip.

'My hour with the drill finishes in ten minutes,' came Veka's muffled voice. 'I'll break then.' Her laser drill began to flare and Jily caught Osip's eyes, winking. They turned and went up the steps and the drill flared behind them. In the control area they stopped. On-screen, Angharad was waiting for them.

'Progress?' Her lips were painted a holographic red and flashed a sweet smile. She knew we were breaking off, thought Jily. Corp really does have this place monitored.

'Two metres in,' said Osip.

'And what's that, a souvenir?'

Osip held up the piece of gold-rock in his hand. 'I was going to check the gas content.'

'Parthenope's notes will give you all that data.'

'They're locked in the computer,' said Osip.

'Yes. We're still looking for her personal code-word—'

'Doomfire,' said Jily. She hadn't meant to – the words just formed on her tongue and popped out of her lips. Angharad's blue eyes looked at her and the hologram fingernails played together. Osip turned to his console and as he did, a new voice spoke.

'Wait.'

Somebody else had stepped into the screen. It was the person who until now had stayed out of sight. He was very senior, even to Angharad. He was tall, broad-shouldered and his blond hair was cut straight and level round a square, firm face. His face was that brown, suntanned colour with a cosmetic speckle of large silver dots on his left cheek. His level, bright black eyes looked at them carefully.

'My name is Herilbert.' He had a deep but oddly emotionless voice, even sexless thought Jily, as though there was no life to it. He was dressed in the dark green tunic and slacks of a World Councillor and the single gold hexagon on his high collar showed he was of the inner circle. Never mind breaking JOKS, thought Jily, this is one of the people who make and break planets.

Angharad had already turned and her slim hands were flickering over a console. The hologram finger-nails flashed busily, and behind them the computer screens hummed.

'Doomfire?' He was looking at Jily, who wished she'd kept her mouth shut.

'I saw it written on a scrap of paper,' she said. It was a lie. Herilbert knew that and so did she, but she didn't want to talk about that desperate scribble on the iron-glass because it meant thinking painfully about Andi again.

'A very lucky guess,' smiled Herilbert. I know you are telling lies, my girl, that smile said, but for now it doesn't matter. Angharad had rejoined him with a very slight nod.

'Can we look now?' said Osip.

'No need,' said Angharad. The red-painted smile was firmly in place. There were bird-wing patterns on her fingernails today, Jily noticed. 'We already have.' And already transferred the data, she thought.

'Are we right about the gas content?' said Osip. He was tense beside Jily – she could feel it, and the little pattering feeling in her stomach began again.

'Yes.' Angharad's smile remained exactly the same.

'You have done very, very well,' said Herilbert. He made the words sound like a row of award certificates. The wide mouth crinkled, but his bright eyes moved between them and Jily turned. Veka had appeared at the top of the stairs and advanced to the centre of the room, both hands cupped in front of her. 'I've found something,' she said.

'Show us, child,' said Herilbert gently. But his big brown hands came together and Jily noticed the right one was speckled with silver in contrast to the left cheek. Veka looked from him to Angharad, puzzled and oddly scared as she opened her hands to show everyone what she held.

Something impossible. Jily could not believe it because above their heads raged non-stop hell-flames that baked Venus into a lifeless burning crust. What Veka showed them explained so much about the coolness, the gas in the rocks; all save the strange cat and mouse game Corp was playing with them. But still impossible for Veka to be holding this stuff, because hell could not freeze.

A handful of ice.

7   *Ice-fire*

'They might've shown a bit more interest,' said Veka with an angry toss of her red head. 'Natural phenomenon!'

'I think they were interested,' said Osip.

His gaze caught Jily's as though by accident. She remembered Herilbert's expressionless face and how Angharad hid her hologramic fingernails in a tight clasp. Oh yes, they were interested and although the screen was smoothed out in glossy blueness, Angharad and Herilbert would still be watching. Corp had this base under an unwinking scrutiny.

Veka's laser drill gouged out the last chunk of red-grey gold-rock, exposing a full archway of glistening ice. Osip took the drill and began chipping out the ice in the pattern of a curved doorway. He stopped and rubbed his wrists a moment, then kicked hard. The slab of ice fell forward like the crust from a pie and crashed to the ground. Behind it now was another solid face, like ice but bluer and seeming more dense. Jily touched it cautiously; it was as cold as ice, too.

'It isn't real ice,' said Osip. His voice sounded casual and a bit loud; Jily realised he was talking to the unseen ears of Corp.

'Yes.' She tried not to make her own voice too loud. 'But it's no use to Corp – maybe we should dig somewhere else.' That'll have Angharad biting her hologramic fingernails, she thought joyfully. She and Herilbert were just too casual about suggesting they 'go on'. Those two either really don't know what to look for or they're just not giving it away.

'Are you both crazy?' yelled Veka. 'They want us to dig here!'

'You're right, Veka,' said Osip. One eye just flickered a little at Jily, but Veka saw it. She shot them both a suspicious look and, grabbing the laser drill, began cutting deeply into the rock. Some ice flew and she snapped her visor down.

'Careful!' snapped Osip. 'If that lot starts to melt, this whole base will flood. We're underground, remember.' Veka nodded and went more slowly. The ice made a pleasant cool tingling in Jily's hands as she carried it over to the scanner. Osip stood beside her as the digital readout flickered. There was a light on the scanner and both had already seen a row of tiny gleaming specks in the scanning lights. New micro-crystal scanners, thought Jily, inset with sound; they'll be in every light through the base. Yes, they're watching us like electronic hawks.

'It seems to be just water and mineral salts.' Osip frowned, looking at the screen. 'But there's a sort of energy layer through it like – like an invisible colour.'

'How come it's so close to the surface and not melted?' Veka called over.

'Maybe that energy structure, I'm not sure. I don't think it's dangerous.'

Jily was turning back to the rock-face as he said this. A chip of the blue ice flew out under Veka's drill and shot straight at her face. She had no time to duck; something small and cold shot between her lips and hit the back of her throat. She swallowed automatically and it tingled down to her stomach. Osip and Veka looked at her.

'Well, if you die we'll know it's dangerous,' said Veka clinically.

Jily swallowed a slightly salty taste in her mouth and waited a moment. 'I don't think I'm going to drop dead, Veka.'

Veka muttered something that sounded like 'pity' and went back to her work. Osip elbowed Jily in the ribs and she grinned, elbowing him back. And in a few minutes she realised that she was feeling a lot better, as though something cool and strong had flooded into her. Even her headache was gone.

There was only room for one at the ice-face. Jily and Osip stacked ice for an hour and then Jily took over from Veka. The red-haired girl hung on to it for a moment, scowling. Lucky I didn't wander into her dream-clip when she was Empress of Russia, thought Jily. She'd probably have had me thrown into a dungeon full of rats.

Her hands were ice-cold and her tunic wet by the time the musical notes of workbreak sounded. She was cutting out a big block of ice and it fell, splintering into gleaming chunks.

'Cut power,' said Osip.

Jily thumbed the controls. Her wrists ached and she stepped back, panting as the cold hit the back of her throat. The ice-face was a jagged deep semi-circle around her. Osip and Veka were loading the ice into a trolley and he straightened with a small piece in his hand. He took it over to the scanner.

'I'm getting a chlorophyll readout.' He magnified it on the scanner. There were tiny specks of green imprisoned in the ice. 'Plants mean the sun once shone on the surface of Venus.'

'What does our botany graduate think?' Angharad's purple smile went in Veka's direction and Jily remembered the top-of-the-class remark.

'Scraps too small to identify with our equipment.' Veka shrugged, very superior. 'And I don't think Corp's looking for frozen vegetables.'

Angharad smiled again. 'Keep a sample.' She had a contrasting gold strip and purple-tinted curls. 'You have all been classified grade H.'

'H!' The first pleased reaction Jily had seen spread over Veka's face. It took two years at Spoke to do that and the cadet was in line for senior posting. She felt stunned when she thought about it.

'That's . . . wonderful.' Osip sounded stunned, too.

'You deserve it.' Angharad's hand was already reaching for the control button. Her fingernails were rubies into sapphires, into emeralds, Jily noticed. 'Goodbye for now.' The screen went blank. Does she *live* in that office, thought Jily?

After dinner, Veka went straight into her cubicle and pulled the curtain without even a goodnight. They heard her dream-cap go down. She's probably Cleopatra flogging the slaves to build pyramids in her honour at being upgraded, whispered Osip, but Jily didn't smile. Those grades were a bribe to keep them working. Osip pushed a cup of hot tea into her hands and Jily flinched a moment. Had Andi handled that cup before her?

'Better get some sleep,' he said, and did a quick circle round his watch. Jily nodded. Osip's circle meant wait an hour for dream-caps.

She was very tired and lay fighting sleep for that hour. She was thinking about Andi, still a private memory she couldn't even share with Osip. And for the unseen Corp watchers, she had to toss and turn and pretend to be sleepless. She wanted to live on Earth and she wanted to explore the galaxy. And she wanted to lose that little feeling inside that said Jily, all this is very wrong. She heard Osip's dream-cap go down and made herself count slowly to one thousand. She liked Osip and her body tingled nicely when she thought of him; she wanted to see him now. Jily stopped counting and pulled the dream-cap down.

There was no need to concentrate this time. She was standing in Osip's dreamstate even as the close screen of the cap brushed her eyelashes. He was standing by his black horse and swung round, startled.

'You nearly caught me!'

He swung into the saddle and they cantered side by side for a little time without speaking.

'I've got a Hard Blues music festival clip,' he said. 'I nearly put it on to see if you rode White Pulsar on-stage.'

Jily wasn't listening. She reined in suddenly and looked round. 'This is changing!'

Overhead the sky was a deeper, richer blue, not that computer-enhanced colour. The grass was thick and long and the tree-line ahead was closer. For a moment she sensed there was life watching her from out of all this. Osip reined in beside her.

'Virtual reality is just computer graphics. It can't change,' he said.

'Neither could dream-clips,' said Jily. 'And those green flecks in the ice – Osip, life on Venus and Angharad didn't even blink!'

71

'She's already read Parthenope's data. I think they know what we're looking for.'

'The energy source? It's locked in the ice?' She looked up at the fresh blue sky and smelt the keen edge of living things on the breeze. That wasn't computer-enhanced either. 'So how does it connect with all this?'

'I don't know. An energy surge, a wavelength.'

'And mixing our dreamstates, how can we do that?'

'We can't, Jily.' He looked at her. '*You* can.' She felt a little chill again, like swallowing that piece of ice.

'You got into my dream-clip, not the other way round.'

'Both of them are changing and I think you're doing that, too.'

'How can I? Osip, what's happening?' The words came out more like a scream than she intended. Osip put his hand on her arm and held it there.

'I don't know. You said you've always had a strong mind . . . maybe Venus is making it stronger somehow.' He kept his grip tight. 'Don't be afraid, we're in this together.'

'Aren't you scared?'

'Jily, I'm scared for both of us.' He tried to grin but his black horse pawed the ground uneasily. 'We have to go on and find out what's happening. What that energy source is in the ice.'

'It's my mind, not yours! You're not taking the risks, I am.'

'You have to hang on!' Osip shouted.

'Oh, do I?' Jily swung White Pulsar round and pressed her sleeve-remote. A blinking moment later, the dream-cap lifted and she turned over on her side, upset, eyes tight shut and not moving, the base silent round her. It was stupid to snap at Osip like that and stupid to shut off the dream-clip. But she was scared and annoyed with herself because of it. She shut her eyes and slept.

It was a funny, confused sleep, up and down and seeming to jolt like Nel's shuttle when the systems went wrong. She was dreaming, enclosed in misted soft glass and outside was a forest, dark green, light green, splotched with red and yellow and blue; crazy shapes moved in it, things with long heads and blunt heads, clawed arms and mouths full of sharp teeth. Now the misty soft grass was disappearing and the things were moving towards her, the plant-life closing and tangling around her legs. Then she woke and sat upright, nearly hitting her head on the overhead dream-cap.

The digital wall-clock showed their sleep-time was almost finished. It seemed colder, but the power coil was humming more loudly under the floor and that didn't make sense – the room should have been warmer. Jily shivered as she zipped on her work suit. Osip and Veka were still asleep and she sat on her bed for a moment, blinking and trying to think. Something had woken her, she was sure. Then she heard it again, a sharp rustling sound.

The control area was silent and the screen blank. But again, she felt there were people watching from the Earth-side of that screen, the way snakes watched their victims. And a growing sense of unease flooded through her mind again. She stopped in the centre of the control area and looked round, shivering. Why was it so cold?

Her mind, Osip had said. If it was happening,
then she couldn't feel it. But even as Jily said that,
she knew she could. As though something powerful
and strong was moving under still water. Then she
heard rustling behind her. It came from the mining
chamber door and as she turned, a finger of hot damp
air touched her cold cheek.

The door was open and dark inside.

Jily walked over. That was wrong, because the light
should go on automatically when the door opened.
She stopped, trying to listen to that deep feeling in
her mind. Be careful, it said, but don't be scared.
Jily pushed the door further open and felt the damp
heat coming from below. She walked to the top stair
and looked down into the hot, sticky closeness.

Something was moving below. Then, dark and
half-seen, it came rushing horribly up the steps at
her.

8 Hands from the ice

She opened her mouth to scream and a slimy wet hand slapped over her face. Jily tore it away, yelled, then felt another wet hand wrap round her ankle. She was jerked forward, off balance, and clung to the stair rail, yelling again. Other flapping hands brushed her face and body and now she could see the darkness below, alive with moving shadows. Something green and spotted, thick as her arm, started to curl around her body. She yelled again and tried to pull herself clear.

'Jily!' came Osip's answering shout from outside. He must have generated more light from the control panel because the mining-chamber lights came flickering on and showed Jily the 'monster' attacking her.

The mining chamber was filled with thick green plants, waving, twitching, each seeming to have a life of its own. All of it came from a thick trunk-like bulb in the centre of the room. Every inch of the wall was covered with sticky green leaf-pads and a twitching, rustling tangle of thick green spread like a carpet all over the floor. Osip was beside her now, pulling the tentacle-vines clear of her body. The 'hands' that grabbed her were open leaf-pads and Osip ducked as one reached hopefully for his face.

'It's a type of creeper and it's trying to settle everywhere,' said Veka behind them. Her footsteps crunched on the leaf-pad carpet. 'It must have – must have come from—'

'From those bits of "frozen vegetable" in the ice, you so-called botany student?' yelled Osip. He kicked another clutching leaf-pad from his ankle and Jily felt one trying to settle on her shoulder.

'They're harmless!' Veka flung out one arm and Jily followed her pointing finger. 'They're somehow plugged into the base power.'

Green leaf-hands were slapped firmly over the energy points used to recharge the power tools. Veka went a little white though and so did Jily. Given enough time, the creeper would have drained all the base energy. The room was hot and steamy, with a queer, sweet vinegar smell and water running between the twisted net of green plant stems. Jily realised the plant-life was generating its own heat and melting the ice. Give this enough time, she thought, and all of Purple Zero would be underwater.

'Then we'd better get rid of it,' snapped Veka and wriggled angrily as one of the creeper-hands began groping down the back of her neck.

Her words were echoed a few minutes later by Angharad. She didn't seem very alarmed though, or even interested. Corp must have known about that thing; maybe they just wanted to see how fast it grew before they told us, thought Jily. They stood before the screen and behind them, curious green leaf-arms were growing through the door behind them. 'I'm not surprised it grew quickly,' she said. 'The power coil was charged with solar energy. The next best thing to sunlight.'

'That's what I thought,' said Veka importantly, but

the effect was spoiled by another green pad trying to pull her red hair.

'Get a specimen, then destroy it.' Angharad's lips were orange and her fingernails set with miniature butterflies. 'Regrettable but necessary.'

'Destroy it?' said Jily.

'Yes.' The orange lips smiled again.

'Has Parthenope's data given you any clues about the power source?' said Osip.

'If it had, we would have said so,' replied Angharad in her best just-do-as-you're-told voice and the screen went dead.

'Let's get on with it.' Veka turned round, skipping over the long creepers and moments later they heard her wrenching a laser drill free from the weed-covered rack.

Osip caught the look in Jily's eye and gave a little smile. Neither of them was going to give anything away in front of Corp's glossy, blue, one-way mirror. But the smile said he understood, that he didn't like destroying things either. Then they heard Veka gasp.

Below, in the rustling green-clad chamber, all the twining, waving creeper arms had blossomed into beautiful blue and gold flowers like orchids. Veka was standing there, still trying to pull the laser drill away, looking round her. Other blossoms appeared on the leaf-pad walls and ceiling, red, purple, yellow and orange, small ones, large ones, drooping upside down from the ceiling and pushing themselves up in clusters from the floor. They waved around on the creeper arms in the middle of the room and a row of small golden blossoms appeared up the stair-rail. A set of large scarlet ones appeared on Veka's creeper-tangled drill and she let go with another incredulous gasp, rubbing her hand over her face. A large smudge of red pollen appeared on one cheek in startling contrast to her pale face. She tried to wipe it off and it rubbed into a larger patch.

'Venus must have been a paradise once,' whispered Jily. A very little blue and red orchid came out on the rail under her hand and she touched it gently. By the ice, a clump of yellow and orange blossoms came out, so dazzling that Jily shut her eyes for a moment. 'It's too beautiful to destroy.'

'So we let it take over the base?' Veka tore the laser drill free and snapped the flaring tongue-flame into life. She swung it round and the orange-yellow blossoms dropped to the floor. 'They're just flowers, Jily.'

She grinned, swinging up the laser and the point flared into the ice-tunnel roof, forming a cavity. Water trickled down and Veka stepped aside. It was right where the dark overhead root-lines were and the melted ice exposed a strip of red. With a cracking sound, it came loose and snaked round Veka's arm, pulling tight. The drill sailed off into the undergrowth and she was nearly jerked off her feet. She yelled.

'Just flowers, Veka?' said Osip.

He grinned and went down the stairs to help her. As he pulled the tendril clear, the ice-tunnel's ceiling fell in with a shattering crash. Hundreds of the long root-things came tumbling out like live, lashing snakes of green, red and yellow. Straight away Jily felt in deadly danger. There was nothing beautiful and gentle about these things – they were unfreezing into a horrible, fast-moving life.

One set of tendrils snaked like a multicoloured hand round Veka, slamming her back against the ice-face. She slid down, apparently stunned, and Osip grabbed for the laser drill. More of the tendrils snatched it from his fingers and others wrapped round his body.

'Jily – the power!' he yelled.

Jily was already halfway down the stairs to help them. But more of the tendril-things were already snaking past Osip and up the stairs at her. They whiplashed together as they did, braiding themselves into thick, strong multicoloured tendrils. She turned to run back up the stairs and one tendril snaked past, ripping off the orchid heads – it was trying to get to the door ahead of her!

Jily dived forward and grabbed the handle. She slammed it shut as the tendril-head rammed against it. More of the things were coming up the stairs and the one at the door reared at her. Jily threw herself off the landing into the orchid jungle below. Osip and Veka were almost wrapped in the things. She had to get to the control console! She landed with a crash and rolled sideways as something looped overhead.

The control-circuit – which one? 'Osip, which one?'

Another multicoloured tendril looped round her wrist. It was like a squeezing steel band of tiny hooks, ripping through the sleeve of her overalls.

'Osip!'

Osip was trying to speak but some red and purple wire was round his neck. He tried to point and another tendril grabbed his arm. Jily rolled sideways again, seeing the tentacles at the top arching over the stair-rail towards her like a multi-headed snake. She was at the control board now, the line of switches in front of her. A thick steel green and purple tentacle wrapped round her body and squeezed crushingly tight. As it did, Osip's screaming words ripped into her head – blue, *blue* and with her last strength she forced forward and smashed her hand into the blue button. The lights fused and everything went black.

Now in the darkness, she could hear the coil-things snaking and heaving. The crushing, squeezing grip round her waist grew even tighter and another began winding round her legs. She could hear a rustling crackling sound and she yelled in desperation, into the darkness: 'Osip! Veka!'

She thought she heard a strangled noise through the rustling. The grip round her waist seemed to be weaker and already the room was colder. Loss of power, loss of heat – they're unstable mutants, she thought, this *must* work! Then the squeezing coil round her waist seemed weaker and the one wrapped round her legs relaxed and fell off. Jily put both hands on the braided tendril and pulled it hard. Her hands became sticky in the darkness and the thing fell off. Ahead of her, somebody gasped.

'Stand still, it's weakening,' said Osip in a choked voice and Jily felt her eyes fill with tears. He was alive!

'Veka . . .' she said.

'All right, I think.' Osip choked again and now, in the blackness, there was a sickly tinge of rotten leaves. 'The big ones all went for you, Jily.'

Jily walked forward. Thick round things still tried to entwine round her legs but she kicked them clear. Somewhere in the crushed mass under her feet were those wonderful flowers too, but she couldn't think about those. Quite suddenly she bumped into somebody – Osip.

'It's OK, Jily.'

They clung to each other for a moment, but a thick rotten smell was already growing stronger. Osip was supporting Veka's limp body and the girl was already beginning to moan and move a little. Jily put Veka's other arm over her shoulder and supported the girl while Osip felt in the darkness for the keyboard. She shivered as a cold wave of air from the ice-tunnel hit her and choked again on the horrible smell. The darkness and the rotting stench seemed to be growing more thickly round them. Osip spoke beside her, also choking.

'We'll have to take a chance.'

The yellow light outlined green-brown masses of rotting undergrowth. The orchids were limp rags and the multicoloured tendrils limp and unwinding from each other. At the end of the tunnel, a thick clotted lump of vegetable matter had fallen out of the ice, the roots sticking in the air. They were curling and turning brown as she watched.

'Come on,' said Osip.

Veka was managing to walk now and her eyes were open. They helped her up the stairs and all three were nearly choking by the time they reached the top. The steps squished underfoot and the stair-rail was wet and slimy to touch. Osip jerked the door open and they stumbled through. Jily breathed fresh air and the control room spun round her for a giddy moment. They let Veka slump into a chair and kicked the door shut without looking back.

It was impossible, though, not to smell the heavy stink of decay or look at each other. Their work suits were torn to pieces; they were cut and aching and smeared with the black rotting goo. Jily rubbed her hand over her hair and felt it plaster down with slime.

'You saved us,' said Osip.

Jily just stood there a moment, not giddy any more, and took a deep breath. She picked up one of the control chairs and swung it around. Jily was a strong girl and rage made her stronger. The chair flew across the room and hit the glossy blue screen.

'Angharad!' she screamed.

9 Gobnait

Jily stood naked in the narrow shower cubicle, her eyes shut as hot water and soap squirted at her from several directions. She rubbed the soap all over her body and pressed a second square metal button. Cool water squirted briefly and she rubbed it off. I bet Angharad never showers from a rationed water-supply, she thought, and it made her angry again. She pressed the hot button a second time but a red light flashed to remind her she'd had her allowance.

Jily sighed and pressed the 'dry' button. Hot air hissed on her wet body and she turned round and round, getting dry but not feeling clean; the shower wouldn't respond to her voice command for another eight hours. Jily walked out into the living area and over to her bunk. Veka was asleep on her bed and Osip was re-programming the circuits in the control area, but that didn't matter. On Moonbase, nobody cared about naked or half-naked bodies except when Corp turned the heating down to save power. She put on her sleep-robe and sat down at the table with a cup of tea. Everything in the last hour was crowding like a succession of different images, slipping into change the way Angharad's hologramic patterns changed on her fingernails.

It had all started when she threw the chair against the wall.

*   *   *

There had been flowers on Angharad's fingernails when she appeared, violets into daffodils and primroses. But the pattern was half-finished, as she hadn't been expecting them. And when they told her what had happened, there was a moment of real emotion in her eyes – fear.

'We want to know what's happening here,' Jily had yelled. 'We want to know everything!'

Angharad's smile had gone quickly back into place. 'None of us know everything.' She disregarded the upturned chair on the floor. Then, 'I realise how upset you must be,' in a tone of voice that really said 'don't get out of line, JOKs.' Angharad's blue eyes had the full authority of Corp behind them and Jily had felt suddenly vulnerable until Osip spoke beside her.

'We want some answers.' He took a step up to stand alongside Jily and she was never more grateful. 'We've met two life-forms and one of them tried to kill us.'

'Not possible,' said Angharad, smiling with dark-blue lips.

'It is possible. It happened.' And this time it was Veka who spoke. She was still sitting down, still dazed, and Jily noticed with a shock that there was blood mixing with the pollen smudge on her cheek. Veka must have hit her head harder than they thought, but the hazel glint was back in her eyes. Even boosters didn't like being pushed too far.

Angharad looked from one to the other. Her blue eyes were expressionless now, but she nodded. 'I'll take the matter under advisement.'

'We're not starting work until you do,' said Osip.

'Then clean yourselves up,' said Angharad sweetly. 'I can just about smell you from here.' Then her smiling image merged back into the glossy blue.

Jily and Osip had gone down into the mining chamber first. Veka joined them a few minutes later, a bandage around her head, her look daring them to object. The flat, steamy heat had all gone and the chamber was ice-cold, the plant-life dead and rotten – and frozen. 'Unstable mutant,' Veka had muttered.

They were tired and still sick and Jily could feel the pressing coil of that braided tendril round her waist. But they couldn't leave the chamber like this, so they spent the next hours cleaning off the walls, floor, ceiling; packing it into the rubbish chute and sending it up to the surface. And when Veka put some under the scanner, another puzzling little hologram image slotted into place.

'It's got the structure Earth plant-life had about the Creataceous period,' she had said.

'Creataceous – the age of the dinosaurs?' said Osip.

Veka had nodded. Plants like this had been growing on Earth about a hundred and fifty million years ago.

Then they had to strip and clean the equipment. The water on the floor had frozen and they had to chip it off because nobody wanted to use laser drills in a skating-rink. And Jily kept thinking about those dinosaur-age orchids and their beautiful blazing colours and how much Venus must have changed in all that time. And the dismissive cold way Angharad had told them to destroy it.

And another little puzzle-image after that – one

that was so terrifying that she hadn't been able to tell anyone about it yet.

'Jily, check the outfall, make sure that stuff is clear.' Osip had been giving her odd looks as he worked. There was something he wanted to say but it would have to wait for their dream-caps.

She had gone up the steps into the astrodome. The scarlet blast of the surface was a welcome reminder of the real world above that strange, close atmosphere below. The chute was clear and as she watched, the lock opened and a last chunk of dead black matter shot out, vanishing in a red flash. Jily felt herself flinch for a moment. Kana had bought her a real Earth flower for her twelfth birthday, but it had died; it was hard keeping Earth flowers alive on the Moon, Kana had said. Jily was hot and flushed from the fire-storms, but that cold prickle kept coming on her skin. Even killing that weed stuff was wrong, she thought – it was just trying to live. We're all trying to live and she traced her hands over the two scrawled words, 'Andi' and 'doomfire'.

Then she had rubbed them out and straight away felt ashamed of herself. She was removing Andi's last presence and the painful memory was still too private to share, even to let her cry. Nothing left of Andi now; the base Copies, directed from Earth, would have put all personal gear in the chute. Nothing back on Moonbase either and no trace anywhere in the solar system. Jily's head pounded as the red surface flared and simmered round her but she couldn't cry.

Now the dust-storm was waning a little and she pressed a button to operate air-jets round the dome. Solid crusts of dust fell away and Jily looked up at the overhanging cloud that imprisoned the poisonous burning atmosphere below like a thick solid ceiling.

Then something flashed as it broke through the orange mass. She glimpsed a pale, metal underbelly, reflecting red against the surface, short stubby wings and red light glinting on bulging eyes. It skimmed along the cloud-cover like a fish across the bottom of a pond, then dived sharply back up into the orange murk.

Jily stood rigid, looking up. She had seen something like that before – the stubby body and bumble-bee eyes were unmistakable. That spaceship that Nel tried to convince her was only a tel-spark. A Betel spaceship, over the surface of Venus? Or something else? The pounding in her head grew worse and she flinched as Osip's voice crackled in the intercom.

'Clear?'

'Yes, clear.'

She had gone below. The cleaning was finished. She knew Osip was looking at her pale face, but she ignored him. They went upstairs and Osip half-paused in front of the screen, but it remained blue and coldly blank.

'I'll get all the lighting-circuits reset,' he said.

So Veka and Jily came through to the sleeping area – Veka straight into a shower, tearing off her clothes as she did. She came out less than a minute later, cleaner, with the red criss-cross weals of tendril-weed over her body. Nor had she bothered with her sleep-robe, just pausing, naked, to look at Jily and utter one flat sentence.

'Thanks for saving me.'

Then she had flung herself on her bed, pulled up the cover and shut her eyes.

*   *   *

Now Jily had taken her shower and she still didn't feel clean. So she drank her tea and went to her own bed. She heard Osip come in, but lay there with her eyes shut, thinking. She heard him get into his bed and she sat up, pulling down her dream-cap. This time she clinically watched herself and she felt the power surge from her mind, that somehow misted the hologram computer enhancement into another reality. It's like the elevator in Moonbase stopping outside two levels at the same time, she thought, and mixing them together, projecting Osip into her own space.

Osip took one look at her face and said nothing. They galloped together over the green grass – thicker and longer than last time – until Jily reined in and buried her face in White Pulsar's mane, breathing in the deep, warm horsebody, to remove the last traces of that dead plant smell from her nose and throat.

'I'm sorry,' she heard him say. She knew he was reaching out his hand, but kept hers firmly gripped on the reins.

'We killed those beautiful flowers.' Jily kept her face in the thickness of the mane but knew her voice was shaking.

'Don't forget those weed-things, Jily.'

She raised her face and looked at him. 'Corp had already told us to kill everything.' She knew a tear was trickling down her cheek, but refused to wipe it away. 'So we did it.'

'We had to—'

'Osip, that makes us no better than Copies! Worse, because they can't think.' Her voice was shaking again, but with rage. 'So what happens if we find something that's flesh and blood?'

'Impossible, Jily!' he shouted with a scared edge to his voice.

'*Venus* is impossible! So is everything that's happening to us right now!'

Osip was still holding out his hand and Jily took it. They nudged their horses closer together and the shaking inside her began to go away. 'I heard your thoughts,' she said. 'When the plant-thing attacked us, you told me which button to press.'

Osip nodded. 'Your mind is getting stronger. I think that helped you face Angharad today, too.'

'You backed me up.'

'I wouldn't have chucked a chair at the screen.' He dismounted and so did Jily. Their hands found each other again in a tight warm clasp and Jily stepped a little closer. Osip gave another of his nice shy grins.

'They might leave us on Venus.'

'No. Corp needs us. Right now we're more important than even Gobnait.' Against her uptight feeling, Jily had to smile. The President of Corp, one of the most powerful people in the solar system? 'I'm serious, Jily. We can find their power source and there's something they don't know.'

'Me?' Osip had touched her gently on the head.

'Something on Venus is doing this to you, and it must be connected to that energy. Maybe that piece of ice you swallowed. And if we find their power source, they don't dare hurt us.'

He was so serious she had to smile again, then laugh. 'Yes, then we'll bang Nel on the head and fly her shuttle to Mars. Nobody likes Corp there.'

Osip grinned too. 'You bang Nel on the head, I'll watch.'

Jily laughed. She put her arms round Osip and let his go round her. Now they were both laughing and they were so close that their lips couldn't help but touching; then they kissed and Jily felt something more wonderful than any power surge through her body. Corp and even the World Council were just names that couldn't reach them. They kissed again and Osip squeezed her tight and swung her round. So she squeezed him just as tight and swung him round and they fell over in the grass. White Pulsar and Black Solar looked down with little whickers of amazement. Then through the whicker came a high, faraway squawking noise.

They sat up and looked over. A flight of black specks was rising from the distant tree-line. Jily scrambled to her feet and Osip followed. 'Jily, does your dream-clip have birds in that tree-line?'

'No.'

The black specks had disappeared now, but Jily felt her fear and unease return. There was other life in this dream-clip and she took Osip's hand again, tight, because that was impossible.

Like everything on Venus.

Veka was still quiet the next morning. She had changed the bandage on her head and just nodded when Osip asked if she was all right. They put on new work suits and when the start-work chimes sounded, they went out and stood in front of the glossy blue screen. Veka frowned a little as though having second thoughts, but took her place with Jily and Osip. The screen came on at once.

'Second thoughts, I hope,' said Angharad in the voice of sweet reason. But she hadn't changed her fingernail pattern or make-up, Jily noticed; somebody's been at work all night, she thought.

'No,' said Osip. 'We want to know what's happening.'

Jily nodded and after a moment, so did Veka. Angharad looked carefully from one to the other. Her smile was just as careful.

'Not from me,' she said. 'The President of Corp.'

All at once she sounded very junior. Then the screen flashed into another image and they were looking at Gobnait.

10   Parthenope's curse

'My name is Gobnait.' The person speaking was seated in a polished, black steel chair with no other furniture in sight save a console on a stand. The voice was low and husky, and seemed neither male nor female.

Gobnait was short and thickset, but with a solid, strong grace. A thin, image-enhancing strip covered both eyes and above it two well-marked black eyebrows rose on either side. Gobnait's head was bald and pink and the chunky hands looked able to fight battles. There was no cosmetic decoration or jewellery and the President of Corp wore a plain blue track suit, like any off-duty miner at Copernicus. Jily realised she knew nothing about Gobnait except the name.

'My voice comes from inhaling magnesium dust at the Ayltus crater.' Jily had heard about that mine; it was before they had Gobblers and was now closed. 'Yes, cadet, I started like you.'

'Cadet' was not said patronisingly, but as a label. That voice was used to labels, probably with price-tags on them, thought Jily. And nor did Gobnait have to explain about his voice. It was his way of saying he did not care about what they knew because he was too powerful to care.

'We sent an unmanned probe to Venus ten years ago, with four Copies. Corp obtained the mineral rights to Venus because our competitors did not consider it economical. We did, because of a special new insulation strong enough to withstand the fire-storms of Venus and called by its colour: purple.' Godnait spoke without moving and it was difficult to tell if the eyes behind those image-enhancing strips were looking at them. 'So we sent an unmanned probe to Venus ten years ago, with four Copies. Their function was to install an insulated mining probe. The first base failed and a second was set up where you are now.'

Then, duty done, the Copies would have quietly melted, thought Jily. Even though Copies were only alloy skin, rods and circuits, she felt a tiny chill at Gobnait's dispassionate tone, like the Moonbase doctor telling Dar he was overweight. 'The probe drilled for a year and took a sample of Venus to the core. There were the minerals we expected to find – and something else.' The doomfire, thought Jily, and Gobnait's screened eyes mind-read into her own. 'Doomfire, trapped in ice, a frozen new energy force waiting to be melted.'

Osip, we were right! thought Jily. She had forgotten about Angharad and Herilbert. The candle flame of their power was nothing to the intense solar light that came from Gobnait. He began speaking again, hands clasped over his stomach like one of those old statues of the Earth Bhudda.

'The energy traces found were heavily diluted in the ice and made up less than a kilogram of solid fuel. It defied analysis.' The strong pink hands unclasped. 'Non-radioactive, very clean – and that one kilogram ran Copernicus for a year.'

Copernicus, thought Jily. Our base has been running on Venusian energy.

'Your Venus shuttle also ran on doomfire. That is why you completed the journey in such a short time.' Gobnait paused again, but all three knew better than to interrupt. Despite the flat tone, there was something about how Gobnait spoke. Interrupting him would be like sticking something metal into a live power point. 'Parthenope found the power source and made a bargain – to mine the energy in return for a very high position in Corp.' Gobnait's lips moved in a very peculiar little smile. Did that perhaps mean Parthenope wanted Gobnait's job?

'Parthenope demanded complete control over the base construction. It was expensive in Copies.' A lot of Copies melting on the surface of Venus before the base was enclosed, thought Jily, but Corp would not care. 'You see, Parthenope knew something about the energy source, something vital, and was therefore able to make these demands.' The hands clasped again. 'Three Junior Operatives were sent – Parthenope wanted no spies and children were easy to dominate. Then three more, yourselves the best we had. Then came the rockfall.'

And death, the end of Parthenope's ambitions. Jily shivered and realised that Gobnait was looking at her.

'What do you know about Venus, Jily?'

It was even more of a shock to hear her own name spoken by that husky voice, that image-scanning look directed at her. She heard herself answer in a voice that tried not to be tiny and scared – and came out sounding exactly like that.

'Just – the briefing clips.' The words clattered like skittles. 'And there's no life here. Now.'

'No life *now*. Because many millions of years ago,

95

all life stopped. It's not enough to have the energy fuel of Venus. We have to know why life stopped.'

'Why is that important?' she heard herself asking.

'Osip, what do you remember about Earth?' Gobnait had turned away from Jily, but she sensed her question was being answered.

'I remember the wide streets and the animal parks. My parents took me there. The little places to eat and the big places to have fun. There were green fields and you could ride animals over.'

'Yes.' The hands unclasped again like the jaws of a trap opening. 'But in a few short years, all has changed. The cities are enclosed and the oceans are nearly dead. We need enormous energy boosts to run the installations that will clean our planet. Much more than we can get from Mars or the Asteroid Belt. We need this energy, children. We need to locate it as soon as possible so full-scale mining can begin. We need to reverse the damage on Earth. We need your skills and courage to go on working until the shuttle comes back.'

'And the Betels?' She hadn't meant to say it, but the words scrawled themselves in her mind like the 'doomfire' letters inside the astrodome. Gobnait took the image-enhancing strip off and looked directly at her.

Once Jily had been working in a Moonbase hangar when a rocket engine was suddenly tested. The sudden roar and flash of hot exhaust fumes made her throw herself down. It was like that now, but without that burning roar. And the same impulse to throw herself to the floor as a pair of tired, blue-grey eyes looked at her like twin lasers.

'Jily, the Betels do not exist. They are rumour.

There is no alien life-force in the solar system.' The soft husky voice did not alter but the words seemed to scorch themselves through her head. She flinched and dropped her gaze, and when she looked up the image-enhancing strip was back in place. 'Now have we told you enough?'

'Yes, sir,' said Veka meekly. She had stood there unspeaking, wide-eyed and open-mouthed, Gobnait's words beating on her like the energy force of Venus. Jily could feel it too, and the personal intense magnetism that made the hologram alive even though Gobnait was millions of kilometres away on Planet Earth.

'Any more questions?' The tone said plainly there would not be. So it was too late to talk about the Betel spaceship, even if she wanted to.

'Corp knows you will be strong.'

The screen flickered and went to glossy blankness and Jily blinked, feeling suddenly lonely and cut-off. Osip rubbed his hands over his face and looked at her.

'Do you want to talk about this?'

'There's nothing to talk about,' snapped Veka. 'Corp has told us what to do – let's do it.'

She turned and marched across the room and through the door. They heard her boots clatter noisily down the steps. Jily shrugged.

Osip paused at the consoles a moment and punched in a general information code. He selected 'names', 'origins of,' and inputted 'Gobnait'. A moment later the line of data read out across the screen.

'Gobnait, Irish, Gaelic, Feminine,' were the first words Jily read and because Osip managed a smile, so did she.

Veka's 'sir' was a woman.

Every work-shift the tunnel went several metres deeper, but they seemed no closer to anything. There were still specks of plant matter in the ice as though scattered by an explosion, but all of them went up the chute. And the further they cut in, the more a sense of urgency gripped Jily and held her tight. There was a feeling of something stealing gently through her brain, and the more ice they cut into, the more that feeling grew. There were no more telepathic moments, but something was getting stronger and stronger, pulling them in.

Now the ice was a silvery blue colour with pale tints of gold flame. It was more difficult to cut and the feeling grew stronger, as though a strange audio signal was pitching itself to her mind-wavelength. She didn't know if Osip or Veka felt it, but the signal made her work harder.

Jily was too exhausted each night to put her dream-cap on and so was Osip. So they had no chance to really talk, but neither would that wonderful kiss become dream-clip memory. They had little secret contact because Corp was always watching; their hands 'accidently' meeting and quick little glances between them. Once Osip traced a heart in a misty piece of ice, then rubbed his hand over it. Jily wished she had told him about the spaceship-thing she thought she'd seen. But not talking like this was good, too, and it kept her warm, working in the cold darkness of the tunnel.

Veka worked even harder than Jily and Osip. Her red hair was pulled back in an untidy knot on her head and the sweat patches under her arms never went away. She handled the laser drill with all the precision intensity of a Copy, chopping out neat chunks of ice. When Jily and Osip's turn came, she would nudge them away until Osip ordered her to stop. Then she chucked ice into the chute with a concentrated fury and always tried to get back to the ice-face as soon as possible. She's being driven, thought Jily, making her body like iron and trying to keep a lid on her emotions.

And when they finished work, they lined up, stained and aching, shivering in their cold damp work suits, and Angharad would flicker into life on the screen like the genie from the lamp – beautiful direct authority, representing everything that was paradise on Earth, always in a different costume, different colours and a smile on her painted lips. It was a strong smile, always sincere and encouraging. Herilbert appeared once and said the same encouraging words, his seagull eyes going from face to face. But Angharad was always waiting, at the end of each shift, and her fingernails went from butterflies to jewels, to leaf patterns and even tiny exquisite snow crystals.

That night, Veka ate her dinner in the usual silence and then said suddenly, 'I'm going to paint my nails like that every day,' and Jily knew she was thinking of Earth and paradise. Veka's hands were red and sore like hers and even under the heavy work gloves, the nails were chipped and broken.

Now they were twenty metres deep in the tunnel and the ice was becoming more difficult to cut. It was denser and a deeper silvery blue and Veka struggled to tear the chunks out, not caring about her fingernails. Jily wanted to contact Osip in the dream-clip but he was always last in from the control area and try as she might, she could not keep awake. The same tight feeling that pushed Veka was pushing her, as though a magic dark secret waited for them behind the ice. And they had to *find* it before Nel came back with an army of Copies. So she fell asleep as soon as her head hit the pillow. Once she was asleep before she had done up the straps. Next morning she was floating against the ceiling and had to push herself down, but nobody laughed. There was nothing funny on Purple Zero.

They had found one more root mass of the red and green wire-weed and chopped it up into frozen sections, sending them all up the chute. When Jily worked at the ice, it seemed to glisten with mocking life and the broken surface reflected their own distorted faces back at them. And once she had the impression Gobnait was watching from behind the blank screen. It almost made her afraid to share another dream-clip with Osip. Could one of the most powerful people in the universe find a way inside and overhear all the secret things she longed to say? Each night she wanted to stay awake and couldn't.

Then, the morning after Angharad's fingernails were geometric patterns of gold and silver, two other things happened on Purple Zero.

Like everything before them, they were impossible.

11 Dreamstate into nightmare

It started when they wrenched a very large chunk of ice free. Veka had been working on it for an hour, getting more and more short-tempered. It had little specks of green-amber running through it. 'Do you want to scan this and see what you're missing, flower-lover?' she snapped at Jily with a bitter, sarcastic smile.

'We scan everything, Veka,' said Osip, chipping a piece off the chunk and throwing it to Jily.

She went up to the scanner and watched as the composite picture grew into detailed life. Just a vine with small flowers, another life-form nobody may ever see again, she thought. Veka appeared beside her and kicked the chute door open. She took the ice-chunk from the trolley but for once her wrists failed her. The block fell with a crash and Veka sank to her knees after it.

'I'll help,' said Jily. She bent over and Veka jumped up, shoving her hard.

'I don't need your help!' She picked up the ice-chunk and slammed it in the chute. She swayed a moment, her eyes half-closed, and kicked the door shut.

'Get some rest,' said Osip.

'I'm all right.' Veka's eyes were open again. 'We've got an hour's worktime left.' Then her voice rose to a jarring screech and her face went white. 'We have to work. You heard the President, Earth is dying!'

'We're no good to Earth, dead from exhaustion,' said Osip. 'Go on, that's an order.' Osip was giving orders more clearly and directly now and Veka glared at him.

'So you can claim the credit, find something – I know you don't like me, I know you whisper behind my back!'

'Don't be crazy,' snapped Jily.

The glitter in Veka's hazel eyes was almost enough warning. Jily ducked sideways, but the other girl's fist hit her on the shoulder and the force knocked her back, against the scanner table.

'You're not going to cheat me – nobody is!'

Jily's shoulder hurt from the blow. She made her own hand into a fist and stepped forward. 'All right Veka, you've been asking for this!'

Veka grabbed one of the laser drills and flicked the point into cutting yellow life. 'I should've been in charge here. I still can be! Gobnait liked me, Gobnait was speaking to *me*, not you!'

'Gobnait needs us all.' Osip stepped up beside Jily and there was a quiet steel in his voice. 'Any trouble now and Gobnait's going to be very disappointed.' He put out his hand. 'You are right Veka, we have to work together to save Earth.'

Veka was still leaning back against the wall, her eyes glaring madly. As Osip held his hand out, she made a flinching movement with the laser. Osip gasped, pulling his hand away, and Veka dropped the laser drill, her eyes still wide but the glaring light going out of them.

'It's all right, I'm not hurt.' Osip curled his hand shut as he spoke. 'Jily, check the outfall. We'll clear up here.'

The outfall didn't need checking and Jily knew it. She also knew Osip was in pain from the clenched way he spoke – but that he wanted to break up the tension in the chamber. So she went up the steps into the astrodome.

The outfall was clear of course. But she stood there a few minutes just to cool down and gave a bitter inside-smile at the thought of it. You couldn't cool down looking at the surface of Venus. The top end of the chute opened a black eye at her and out shot another chunk of ice, vanishing with an explosive hiss. Jily was about to go down when she saw something that made her stop and look at it for a long time.

Something impossible.

'Osip.' She tried to keep her voice natural as she spoke into the intercom. 'There's some blockage, I'll need you or Veka to help with the robotic arms.' Putting it that way would stop the girl getting even more paranoid, but oh, do come yourself Osip, she relayed in her mind, wishing the telepathic powers were back. There was a clatter of magnetic soles on the steps and Osip appeared. He gave her arm a little squeeze and she smiled and put a finger on her lips.

'See the blockage?' she said.

'Yes.' He gave a puzzled look. 'What?'

'I'll put my side out first.' Jily slipped her hand into the control set and extended the purple-sleeved robotic arm with its purple-gloved metal hand.

The metal fingers, as flexible as her own, dug into a pile of red-baked dirt and turned it over. A small metal hub-cap rolled out. They had replaced two wheels on the trolley and sent the worn parts up to the surface. Jily turned the metal cap over and tapped it with her metal fingers. It was made of a heat-resistant alloy but was white-hot.

'I'll try my end,' said Osip, to keep up a pretence for the electronic Corp ears. But his look said – what the hell are you getting at?

Jily turned over the cap again. It was hollow. She tapped it with her metal index finger and left a little dent in the side. Then she crushed the cap under the purple-gloved hand and stabbed a purple thumb up at the howling red wilderness overhead. Osip's eyes went round as he understood and his own long arm extended a purple hand to pick up the squashed cap.

The gravitational pressure of Venus. Osip's purple fingers were digging into the waste and another small cap rolled out. It was white hot and dented by his fingers, but also uncrushed by an impossible pressure of gravity that even flattened rocks! Osip looked at it incredulously, then nodded to show he understood. He extended his own purple-sleeved robotic arm and smoothed a patch of the red waste flat with the purple hand. Then with an index finger he wrote a big 'D'. Jily made a lowering gesture over her face and Osip nodded again. Then, more slowly, the robotic finger digging and scratching the hard, baked waste, he wrote words that chilled Jily.

Drink nothing.

Jily looked at him, but Osip's face was expression-less and when she looked up, his purple robotic hand was already wiping out the words. Then he pressed the retract control, said loudly, 'Seems to be working now,' and left.

*　　*　　*

'Every time I'm back from putting the day's work into the computer, you're asleep. So is Veka. OK, we're all tired but nobody crashes like that.'

They were in Jily's dream-clip and leading their horses. The distant tree-line was much closer, the trees broad-trunked and heavy with branches. The grass was long with little yellow flowers spotted between. And Jily still sensed the impression of life round them.

'You think they're putting something in the water?'

'We didn't drink anything tonight. Veka did.'

And Veka had gone to sleep the minute she was on her bunk, Jily thought. She'd taken some twenty minutes and had to wait for Osip. 'It would make sense,' she said. 'They've told us all their secrets and they want us working – not talking.'

She stopped. For a moment White Pulsar's rein felt light in her hand and she looked back. It was as though a glowing line surrounded the horse for a moment, then faded away again. But she was thinking about the impossible thing that happened a few hours earlier.

'Why didn't gravity crush those hub-caps flat? Osip, it would crush *us* flat!'

Osip was leading Black Solar. He stopped for a moment and tugged the reins as though they'd become light. Then he sighed and shook his head. 'Then it must be changing somehow.'

'All over the planet? Osip we'd know!'

Osip stopped again, the reins limp in his hand. 'Maybe . . . round the base. We're shifting all that ice on to the surface. There are those energy traces in it . . . maybe they're making a clear area.'

'That's impossible,' said Jily, and realised how

stupid her words sounded. They were dealing with an unknown energy source, one that even the Corp labs could not analyse – anything was possible.

'Jily.' Osip pointed at the tree-line.

Once it had been a neat distant line in her dream-clip. Now they were close enough to see them clearly. Jily had seen neat, well-behaved trees in holograms and even a miniature real one. But these were taller than a six-storey moonbase and over-shadowed everything with a strong, unruly pride as though daring humans to challenge them. And at the same moment, the reins went light in her hand again and she spun round. White Pulsar had already vanished and beside it, Black Solar was disappearing in a shimmering haze.

'What's happened?'

'They've been displaced,' said Osip. He took an uncertain step round. 'Whatever force took over your dream-clip has displaced it completely.' He saw her hand go to the little remote on her jacket cuff. 'Do you want to go back?'

Jily's hand stayed on the button but she shook her head. 'Let's find out.'

Osip took her hand and smiled. He's got the best smile I've ever seen, thought Jily, and squeezed his own hand back. The sun beat strongly on their faces and a rich smell of flowers and living green things came to their noses. Jily had never dreamed anything could be as lovely as this. Now the sunlight and leaves mixed in dark patterns and the same shadow spread like a cool cloak round them. Jily was standing under a tall tree, the way people on Earth once did, and it was magic. There was a faint chattering sound somewhere and the sound of movement.

'Life?' she whispered. Life in dream-clip? Now her head was hurting a little and she looked round. There was more slight noise and movement now; as though removing the dream-clip image, they had unlocked into another level of life. Then something moved again and a little thing darted out of the tree cover and settled on an outflung branch. Jily glimpsed a body covered with brown fur, a pointed beak and bright eyes that swivelled to look at them. Then it spread bat wings and leapt out of sight.

'That's not a hologram,' said Osip.

Now one of the branches in the tree seemed to be moving overhead. It was a snake, very long and thick-bodied like a length of olive-green cable patterned with blue rings. A tiny red tongue flickered from lips as thin as Herilbert's and cold yellow gemstone eyes watched them. It paused then turned away, beginning to coil smoothly back round the massive tree-trunk. Osip and Jily realised something at the same time and the cool shadows became cold round them for a moment. Both those creatures had looked at them, seen them and moved away.

And that was impossible.

'They saw us,' said Jily. They moved back out of the shadows into sunlight and began circling round the tree.

'This isn't just another dream-clip.' Osip's voice shook. 'That force is somehow holding this together and integrating us into it, like a live memory recall.'

'How did we become part of the memory?' Some creeper tangled on Jily's foot a moment and she jumped, remembering the wire-weed. This couldn't be happening. Something had circuited into their minds via a simple dream-clip and they were in an alien landscape.

'Venus, when it was alive,' she whispered softly.

They were nearly clear of the trees now. A cluster of brown fruit hung from one branch. The 'fruit' unfolded leather wings and poked long-beaked heads out, then scattered. Some flew and some scrambled back along the branches with tiny hooked claws set in their bat-wings.

'They're like . . . like pterodactyls . . .' said Osip.

'Ptero-what?'

The name rang a bell from her school lessons somewhere. Then she tripped and nearly fell over a large curved rock. The 'rock' blinked offended eyes up at her and tucked head and legs into its shell. Osip had gone a little way ahead, and turned.

'Jily!'

She forgot about the tortoise and ran forward – then stopped, forgetting the pterodactyls and every other strange life-form. Because what was ahead took her breath away.

It was as though a machine as big as one of the giant Moonbase Gobblers had been working for a hundred years in the same place. Or giant hands had scooped handfuls of earth by the tonne for the same length of time. Ahead of them the ground sloped, gently then more steeply, and thick long grass and bushes ablaze with those wonderful orchids. The other sides were lost in the haze of distance and through the bottom wound a sparkling river. The steel-blue waters separated round a little green island, dotted with brown-green logs spilled and tumbled by a flood. And on the river-banks there were huge trees with thick glossy trunks and outspread branches that looked as though they had been growing for hundreds of years. Even the clouds overhead looked fat, white and healthy, not just the cosmetic scribbling of a hologram.

'Osip.' Jily pointed at a dazzling pyramid cluster of red and orange orchids. 'Flowers like those were in the ice and we dated them a hundred and fifty million years . . .'

'To the Cretaceous period,' whispered Osip. 'The – '

A deafening croak sounded and they jumped round so quickly that Jily tripped and fell. A brown-green 'hill' near Osip was moving up out of the thick grass, trailing creeper from a long, long neck, arching skyward and ending in a big blunt-shaped head with a floppy brown crest. Huge nostrils flared over a wide mouth set with batteries of white teeth, and inset piggy eyes flicked in their direction.

'– Age of the dinosaurs,' he finished, pulling Jily to her feet.

The high crest began to stiffen as the head turned; behind, bushes were flattened and a shower of blue orchids scattered as a long tail swished like a giant broom. Then with another loud roar, one huge leg stepped forward and the creature moved in their direction.

12 Wolf-creatures

'Brachiosaurus, I think,' gasped Osip.

'Brakky – what?'

'Brachio – duck!'

He slammed her back to the ground and threw himself down beside her as the long tail came swishing around and flicked with whiplash speed at them. The crest was fully erect now, the eyes glaring and another stump-leg crashed forward.

Osip and Jily scrambled up and ran down the sloping rise. The tail tip whip-cracked somewhere behind them and another loud roar blasted behind them. Osip chanced a look back and stopped.

'It's not following. Anyway they were herbivores, plant-eaters.'

'Maybe it thought we were plants,' panted Jily breathlessly. The 'brakky' was still watching them, the long neck at full stretch. Six storeys high, tall as a Moonbase, thought Jily. 'Osip, can we talk on the move – backwards?'

Osip grinned. 'It's just warning us off. Look!'

Beside the huge bulk of the adult dinosaur was a high clump of something that looked like bamboo. A long neck poked out of it and little bright eyes blinked anxiously at them, the mouth making a high piping sound. Down came the adult's head gracefully on the long neck and a huge pink tongue, the size of a door, licked raspingly up the neck and face of the young one. Baby, thought Jily, and it's three times as big as me.

111

'There!'

His face was alight with fascination as he pointed. In the distance, behind the slow-moving brakky was a small herd of four-legged animals, zebra-striped in green and black. One of them reared up, holding the trunk of a small palm in the strong forelegs while it pushed a square-shaped snout into the green palm-head.

'Hadrosaur – duckbilled dinosaurs!'

'Osip . . .'

There was a slithering in the grass and Jily moved hastily in case another giant snake was crawling towards them. But it was only a red, yellow-spotted lizard that rose up on two powerful hind legs, the front held like paws, and scuttled away.

'Might be a composasaurus—'

'Osip!' Jily felt like punching him. 'What the hell is going on!'

'Sorry, Jily. But this is all so incredible. I've only seen things like this in those reconstruct-holograms—' He broke off as he saw Jily's hand go into a fist and hastily indicated some rocks. 'Let's sit down.'

Jily made sure hers *was* a rock before she did. Osip stood a wondering moment more and looked round at the late afternoon sky. The blue was deeper in the west but the sun still shone like a golden ball; round them, heat shimmering on their faces and bodies, the glorious heat of living energy that Jily had never felt before. She was more breathless than scared. She was hot and slipped off her jacket. Osip sat beside her and touched the sleeve-remote.

'We can zap out any time with this.'

'Are you sure?'

'Find out.' Osip pointed at the remote. 'We're safe with that.'

Jily let her finger touch it. 'You want to find out more, don't you?'

'We have to. But we are safe, Jily. This is in our minds – your mind. Technically we're under our dream-caps on Purple Zero.'

'So what's happening to my mind?'

It all still felt like an unreal sunlit dream and she couldn't keep that little fluttering note from her voice. She folded her jacket carefully and placed it on a rock beside her. She kept one hand on the remote and Osip took her other and squeezed it hard. The crashing sound of the brakky footsteps had died away and there was a deep hush as though everything was getting ready for the night.

'We know what a dream-clip does.' Osip was talking carefully, pausing to think as he did. 'It just feeds the brains a set of messages, telling it what to see, feel, smell and so on. That energy stuff must do the same and it's making its own special reality.'

'Like a replay?' Jily kept her hand on the button.

'Yes. What was that thing happening on Copernicus – the special thoughts people kept getting?'

'Mindspread,' said Jily. The sky was lower now and redder, and the air was still. Moonbase was millions of years distant in the tomorrow, it seemed, and she put both hands on Osip. She felt calmer. 'It just seemed to glitch our circuits.'

'Maybe that's how this energy can get to you.' He sighed.

'Mindspread only affected the young people.' She was looking at him now and didn't notice her folded jacket begin to move. She looked at the west and the setting sun.

'How can we be on Venus? The sun's setting in the west, like Earth does.'

'We are. There's no way we could be on Earth. There must have been similar life development – it's possible.'

'Osip . . .'

Forgetting her jacket, she stood up and pointed. Overhead a moon had begun to come out. But it was much bigger than the moon round Earth and it glowed, full of colour that filtered from behind the clouds.

'That's another planet,' said Osip. 'Venus must have had a . . . sister planet.'

'Then it must have broken orbit a hell of a long time ago,' said Jily. She sat down and poked at a little rose-like flower at her feet, flinching as a thorn pricked her. 'When?'

He broke off and gently took Jily's pricked finger. There was a tiny red speck of blood on it.

'Did you feel that?'

'It's all right, Osip,' she said. 'It doesn't hurt.'

Osip was still looking at her with bewilderment and fear. 'But it happened, you felt that.'

'What's wrong?' She felt a growing prickle of unease.

'This . . .' His voice broke off a moment. 'This energy force has integrated us so fully that we're part of it. We have – we have a separate identity inside it.'

'We can see, hear and feel things.'

'We can be hurt,' said Osip.

Jily remembered the crack of that whiplashing tail.

114

'All right then, let's get out of here.' She stood up again, grabbing for her jacket.

It was no longer there.

The 'rock' she had placed it on was now some twenty metres away and still moving. It was a giant tortoise and while Jily and Osip were talking, had quietly grown legs and walked off, Jily's jacket still neatly folded on top.

'Don't move, Jily,' said Osip softly.

Her first impulse was to run and get the jacket. But she had already frozen before his warning nudge. Neither of them looked at the tortoise as it stopped moving and sank to the ground, tucking arms, legs and head back into the thick rounded shell. They were looking at the reason why it stopped, the reason that stood another twenty metres further on; utterly motionless and caught in the act of stalking them.

A creature out of a nightmare.

Another dinosaur, but two-legged, and standing upright with a tiger-patterned orange and black body, a heavy head and forearms that ended in big, three-clawed hands. The wide half-open mouth showed long, sharp, white teeth. The creature took a step forward and a small shrub suddenly fell underfoot.

'Deino – something . . . I think,' whispered Osip.

A second plant split nearly in two halves as the 'deino'-thing took another step forward and Jily saw why. The creature's strong, thick-muscled legs ended in three-clawed feet and each centre claw was a large white sickle, curved, cruel and very sharp. Osip's whispers became sharp with tension.

'Jily, the Earth version of these hunted in packs.'

And now they could see more yellow eyes glowing, back in the forest cover where the bushes grew thickly. There were yellow glints like hungry flame-eyes on both sides, all round, as more of the two-legged deino-creatures stole out into the gathering twilight. Perhaps they had been stalking the brakky and duckbills for the last kill before night, but Osip and Jily were their prey now. The pack leader took another step, casting a long black shadow.

'We'll have to out-think, out-bluff them!' Osip's low voice was edged with furious thought. 'Change our eye-lines.'

'Osip—' Jily broke off, looking at him. Had Osip gone mad?

'Get on my back – Jily *move*!' He *was* mad, she thought. Osip spoke quickly, the words tumbling out. 'Those things aren't sure about us, we don't key into their visual triggers – get it?' He was ripping two palm fronds from a young tree.

'Like we're food but in a funny package?' Osip nodded as she scrambled on to his shoulders and he thrust the two palm fronds into her hands.

'When we walk towards your jacket, flap those things and make a squawking sound. We'll be over their eye-line, still strange-looking, but maybe they'll pause long enough.'

And maybe they won't, Jily thought, but she dug her knees in and hefted the big palm fronds as he took the first step. He half-muttered something, but in the utter twilight silence Jily heard it clearly: 'Good luck, my love.'

Before she could answer, Osip took the first step forward.

'Squawk!' he hissed.

Jily tried to but the first attempt caught in a

dry throat. She tried again and managed a loud choking howl.

'Flap!' came a tense hiss and Osip took another step.

Jily began to flap the palm fronds up and down like huge wingbeats. Osip was walking steadily, carefully, his arms locked round her legs. Overhead the moon hung brilliant in the dark blue sky. There were more than fifty of the deino-creatures in sight now, the red setting sun casting blood-shadows round them. They were still motionless, yellow eyes like intent beacons, and long stiff tails stuck out sharply behind them. The pack leader was standing, head cocked and on one leg like a bird, sickle claw flashing white in the sun's shadows.

Jily squawk's howled again and the heavy fronds weighed down her hands as she waved them overhead again. I'm doing flying-monster impersonations so we don't get eaten by dinosaurs in my mind, she thought and it was so crazy, she nearly giggled and changed it into another long squawk.

They were nearly at her jacket and still the pack leader hadn't moved. It was the biggest, nearly three metres tall; she could see the sharp white teeth and zigzag of vivid tiger stripes. Behind it, none of the others moved, but their heads pricked up as though puzzled. Osip's foot cracked a dry twig in the tense stillness and Jily covered with a louder squawk. One wrong move, and they'll be on us like wolves, she thought. Then the pack leader put its claw-foot down and the stiff tail seemed almost to quiver uncertainly. It was working! Jily flapped again and squawk-howled at the top of her voice. Hope it's not a mating call, she thought.

117

The other deinos were making little chattering noises that also sounded uncertain. Jily flapped the fronds and her arms ached. This was unreal, it was millions of years ago and shouldn't even be happening, but it was *working*! The jacket was only two steps away when Osip's foot caught in a ground vine and he tripped. Jily crashed down over his head and with terrifying loud screeches, the deinos unfroze and charged forward.

Jily scrambled to her feet, reaching for her jacket. But in sudden horrible bounds, the pack leader was already there, eyes glittering, leaping at her like a nightmare ballerina. One leg stabbed forward and Jily flung herself down again as the sickle claw flashed overhead. She grabbed the jacket, the control at her fingertips, but the deino had already recovered, its foot skidding along the tortoise armour-shell as it drew back. One side claw caught her jacket and whisked it out of reach.

Then it spun round with the same terrible speed and the sickle claw flashed into her face.

13   Aliens of the fire-storm

'Jily!' Osip screamed. He grabbed the palm-frond and whacked the creature as hard as he could. It ducked with agile grace and the sharp teeth flashed, catching the branch, snapping it short. On all sides, the other deinos were running in with a deadly, prancing speed. The pack leader lunged again as Jily dived for her jacket. Her hand over the button, she made her fingers press it as the sickle flashed in, click—

Everything zapped into tiny, bright unfocused lines, dots and zigzags, then she was jerking upright in her bed, her forehead banging against the rim of the rising dream-cap. She lay back, feeling her head press into the pillow. The flat recycled-air smell of Purple Zero was around her, the blue screens on her bed and the purple ceiling overhead. But she was hot and sweaty as though still under the hot Cretaceous sun, her body taut from the memory of those tiger-striped creatures from a prehistoric nightmare. Jily let her fingers slide over her stomach to make sure her insides were not unzipped by that terrible sickle claw. Then she sat up in bed.

'Were you having a nightmare?'

Veka was standing there, concern on her face for a moment before the usual tight scowl returned. Jily just nodded, then got up and ran quickly into Osip's cubicle. His dream-cap was also up and he was sitting on the side of his bed. He gave a tense little grin and tried too hard to be casual.

'Sleep well?'

'You two are using your dream-caps too much.' Veka's eyes were dark with suspicion. 'That can be dangerous.'

'Yes, yes, it can be dangerous,' said Jily slowly, her eyes still on Osip, feeling an absurd desire to giggle. Must be the shock, she thought – better watch that. The musical notes of wake-up were sounding and Veka gave them another frowning look before heading for the showers. Wondering why we go to bed with our clothes on, Jily thought.

She showered, dressed and selected a pancake biscuit for breakfast. But when she bit a piece off, she remembered the deino cracking that branch in its teeth and put the biscuit down. Osip pushed a cup of hot tea into her hands and she sipped it gratefully, aware she was still trembling a little – and that Veka was still giving them frowning, puzzled looks. Then Veka moved away and even with Corp monitoring everything they did and said, she had to speak.

'Thanks.' You saved me, came plainly on the end.

'Thanks, too,' said Osip, his face straight, 'for squawking so loud.'

Jily felt that stupid desire to giggle again. What would the Corp listeners make of that?

'Two together,' she said softly. The listeners would make nothing of that, either. For Jily, though, the memory of that sister planet glowing in the blue Venusian twilight still burned in her mind.

Osip put out his hand and squeezed hers tight. The hot tea was relaxing her and Jily leaned over and gave him a kiss. Corp could see that, too, but so did Veka as she came out with a towel wrapped round her.

'Play your games back at Moonbase,' Veka snapped. 'We've got a tunnel to dig.'

'Jily,' said Angharad. Jily stopped by the screen. She had just finished lunch, a little behind the others, and as she followed them back Angharad shimmered into presence. Her hair was bronze, highlighted with blue and gold, and she had on a silk multicoloured tunic; those wonderful fingernails had a pattern of entwining lines that flowed, circled and squared into rainbow colours every time she moved her hands.

'How are you?' Angharad's voice was as sweet as her bronze-tinted lips.

'I'm fine.'

'Your hard work is very necessary.'

'Yes,' said Jily. And two of us nearly ended up in the jaws of a flesh-eating dinosaur, but you don't know that.

'How is your mindspread?'

The question was so smooth and abrupt that Jily nearly jumped. Suddenly she realised it was very difficult to hide things from those deep blue eyes. 'I'm not getting headaches any more,' she said.

'If anything strange happens – tell us.'

'Yes.' Had she waited a moment too long before saying that? But Angharad's smile stayed just as sweet.

'Anything, Jily. It could be very important.'

Corp must have picked up something, but how much? They would have seen the dream-caps go down together, maybe seen their distress as they lived that dream-clip nightmare. But not even Corp could get into their brains and unlock secrets of the Venusian dinosaur age.

'I'll do my best.' That was true. She and Osip would do their best to find out what was happening.

'We know. This conversation is private, Jily. You're special.'

Angharad's blue eyes stayed on Jily for a long, warm moment before she lifted one hand in graceful farewell and reached for the remote button. The movement – also graceful – made Jily think of the deino's prancing leap as the screen went dead. Oh, nice one, Madam Director, thought Jily, now go and have a big long laugh with all your painted Corpmates about conning the little JOK – and knowing if the little JOK repeats just one word, you'll know at once. And why was *she* special? Jily went below.

Their tunnel angled sharply down a step at the end now, turning a corner. The silvery blue seemed thicker there and Osip had ordered a change in direction. Now the ice-face was glowing a deeper blue with bright sparkles of silver weaving through as though the movement of water and waves had been frozen together. Veka was pulling a trolley of ice-chunks to the chute as Jily joined Osip at the ice-face. They were out of sight of Corp now, but the unseen electronic ears would be listening intently. She glanced back, then drew a big 'A' on the silver blue face and pointed at herself.

Osip rubbed it out and drew a question mark. Jily printed quickly, 'SAYS I AM GREATEST.' Osip grinned, then frowned, pretending not to understand. He wrote another question mark. Jily jostled him, he jostled back and they grinned again. Oh, this is not real, she said to herself; a few hours ago we were being attacked by flesh-eating monsters and now we're playing like kids. Osip rubbed out the marks as Veka appeared again and the girl's mouth set in a straight frowning line that always seemed there now.

'We're slowing down,' she said.

'The ice is getting harder to cut,' replied Osip.

'Maybe you've got your mind on other things,' snapped Veka. 'You both know how important this is.'

She knew Osip was right, though. As the ice became a deeper silver, the laser drills cut upon it much longer before even a groove appeared. Veka almost snatched the drill from Osip.

'My turn now.'

She began working with fierce intensity, not looking at them. Jily helped Osip load the trolley and they pulled it back up the tunnel to the chute. The chunks they loaded in now were almost pure blue-silver and didn't even look as though they would melt. This stuff is not ice any more, thought Jily.

Osip slammed the chute-lock and a moment later they heard it click-thud overhead. 'Veka, we're checking the chute. The outlet may be blocked,' Osip yelled. Veka's answering shout echoed back up the ice-passage. He nudged Jily and together they went up the steps into the astrodome. Osip extended the robotic arm on his side and Jily did the same; a moment later their purple-fingered hands were writing to each other on the red-baked surface of Venus.

'MUST TELL VEKA,' Jily wrote.

Osip wrote a big question mark under this. WHY?

Because Angharad talks to me alone, which means

Corp is trying to split us up. So we must be closer. Jily struggled to put this into big simple letters with her purple writing finger. Outside another dust-storm was rising and the scudding dust made writing difficult, wiping each word as it appeared. There was a little sharp buzzing sound in her mind like an up-down sonic hum. Jily struggled with another word but the dust-wind kept wiping them out. Osip grinned with sympathy but Jily ignored him, trying to write, telling him what was in her mind. He sent his purple hand over the smooth surface and it touched hers. Jily was burning inside with frustration – she wanted to talk about Corp, Veka, everything! Then their purple hands touched and the fingers clasped a moment. Inside the dome, Osip flinched and his eyes blinked wide. *He understood* – he's picked up on everything she said!

Outside the astrodome, their purple-gloved hands, still clasped, were hidden from sight in red, storming dust. They unclasped and retracted the hands and as they did, Jily felt the link end, like an ultrasonic signal stopping. She looked at Osip and he looked back; both were a little scared. We'll be back under our dream-caps tonight; I don't need telepathy to tell Osip that, she thought, and followed him down the steps again. At once she was feeling a surge of high-charged excitement at her sudden new power, but feeling something else when she remembered the expression in Osip's eyes.

Fear. He was scared of her.

'Doomfire,' said Osip, as much to himself as to Jily.

'Do you think that's causing all this?'

Osip just shrugged his shoulders. It was high

noon in the Venusian dinosaur-age, with a shining golden sun directly overhead in a cloudless blue sky. The sister planet was just visible, low on the horizon, as a pale outline. The only evidence of their twilight encounter with the deinos were crushed and claw-chopped plant stems round the rock, already dry in the sun. The deinos were gone.

'Looks like they got something.' Osip pointed down the slope to the river and the torn remains of a dinosaur carcass half in the water. 'One of those duckbills maybe. Now the body will be carried downstream and covered with silt. Then the process of turning it into a fossil will begin. It'll take millions of years.'

'Osip!' Jily didn't mean to sound exactly like Veka, but she was looking round at the same time and was very tense. The deino that nearly caught them had not given any warning.

'They'll have gone on, following the duckbills and the brakkies.'

'How can you be sure?'

Osip was walking a little way forward. He grinned and pointed over to a steaming brown hillock, with blowflies hovering overhead like a buzzing blue-black halo. On the edge of it was a three-toed claw print, the centre claw deeply indented.

'They went thataway,' he said. Then he saw the look on her face. 'Jily, we're safe.'

'Osip, inside or outside my mind we're not safe on Venus.'

A harsh, distant croaking sound had made Jily turn as she was talking. A big but distant version of the pterodactyls was coming down the river, gliding down low. But from that her eyes lifted to the sky again and she stopped, pointing up.

The pale white dot they had seen yesterday was larger now and the size of a small coin. 'Might be a small comet. There was a lot more solar disturbance in those days,' said Osip.

'Those days, these days . . .' Jily shut her eyes a moment; the sun was almost too hot. She opened them and watched as a giant red butterfly settled on the brown pile of brakky dung. 'Why is this happening to me?'

Osip led her over to sit on the rock. Jily sat down on the rock and shut her eyes; all she wanted to do was sleep. Osip knelt beside her, looking round all the time as he spoke.

'Sometimes, somehow, you get into minds. The other day because of stress, today when' – he frowned and thought for a moment – 'when we linked those robotic hands.'

'Coincidence,' said Jily, her eyes still shut.

'Maybe. But what about mindspread on Copernicus? How the equipment sometimes glitched.'

'That happened a year before we came here. And it didn't make us read minds.' Jily still didn't want to open her eyes.

'One year,' she heard Osip say.

'One year,' she heard her own voice reply. 'Anyway if this ultra-real trip is caused by doomfire then how can the two be connected?' She opened her eyes again and almost felt her mind click into focus as Osip went on speaking.

'And for the last year, Moonbase Copernicus has been powered with Venusian energy . . .'

Jily stood up. She wasn't hot any more, she was

cold. 'I was getting little doses of that stuff, "very diluted",' Angharad had said. Now she had a major dose, maybe in the piece she accidentally swallowed. She was shaking a little and Osip put his arms round her. Somewhere in the distance, a set of howling honks echoed as dinosaurs called each other.

'We have to tell Veka,' Jily said.

'Veka—'

'Yes, Veka, she's important—'

'She's a Corp-girl, a booster who wants to get to Earth. And she hates us.'

'Veka is bright and she's tough. She doesn't like us because we shut her out.'

'She hasn't tried to be friends,' muttered Osip, still looking at the comet.

'Neither have we!'

In the distance, the dinosaurs were still calling each other. Another big brown pterodactyl glided over the river, low enough to spear fish with its beak. More of the big red butterflies were circling round and there were some little darting yellow ones.

'Not yet, Jily,'

'Yes!' She'd never felt more certain. 'I'm going to ask her now.'

'Wake her up?'

'She's got her dream-cap on, I saw it.'

'Jily!' Osip gave a horrified yell. 'You can't just go into her dream-clip.'

'I can.' Jily knew her smile was wicked but that energy fire was getting through her body. 'Are you coming?'

She held out her hand. Osip grabbed it and opened his mouth to protest. Jily shut her eyes and a set of wavebands seemed to project through her mind.

Osip's shout faded out and her mind clicked those wavebands together in a single broad dazzling surge of light. Then a sharp, thick smell hit her nose, a mixture of sweat, rubbish, bodies – Jily could still feel Osip's hand holding hers as she opened her eyes.

They were in a wide corridor covered with wood panels, painted in bright crude colours. Before them was a pointed door, also made of real wood, set with iron clasps and guarded by two men, dressed in thick wool tunics of red and black and wearing floppy black bonnets. Each held a long wooden staff with a shaped metal point. Spears of some kind, Jily knew, and she'd never seen so much wood.

She could feel long, uncomfortable clothes all over her body, something thick and clinging on her head. She darted a look at Osip beside her. He had on a shaped tunic of heavy cloth, striped red and yellow and red knee-length pants and white stockings. A red cap with a yellow tassel was on his head; Jily knew she looked exactly the same.

'The dream-clip is compensating, dressing us for Veka's period,' whispered Osip. Sure, Osip, fine, but what *is* Veka's time? thought Jily. That was something she hadn't stopped to consider.

The two guards seemed to know they were there. Both short men with rough-clipped beards, they uncrossed their spears and opened the door. Jily felt Osip's hand still in hers and she held it tightly as they walked through the door.

The chamber inside was wood-panelled and painted like the corridor with a high vaulted ceiling. There were candles set in iron brackets along the walls and shafts of dim sunlight from long windows set with tiny, thick panes of glass in lead. The paintwork was smudged with candle smoke and there was the same hot heavy smell of bodies and scent oils. There were people here, looking at them, then away, with polite detachment. All the women had thick-painted faces and wore their hair up in stiff big curls. All the men wore old-fashioned Earth fabrics, velvet, wool and leather, and some had shaped pieces of shiny metal on their bodies – armour. Their beards were more shaped and they had long pointed moustaches. There was silence in the room and Jily felt a tingle of unease, danger.

She knew they were meant to walk forward, and she knew enough to snatch her cap off as she did. Beside her, Osip did the same and Jily felt for the remote clipped to the sleeve of her tunic. *That* wasn't going anywhere again. Ahead of them, a woman dressed in a full and splendidly embroidered skirt swirled away, leaving the centre of the room clear except for a woman seated on a tall, carved, wooden chair that was covered with thick gold paint.

She was dressed in a full-sleeved, long-skirted garment with a stiff white raised collar. Every inch of the thick purple material was sewn with gold and silver thread and tiny precious stones that winked and glimmered in the mix of candle-sunlight. Her hair was so huge and thick-curled that it must be a wig and she had a long gold stick set with jewels in her hand. And Jily knew that woman, for the big red wig and thick-painted face could hide everything but those blazing hazel eyes. And Veka's voice was the same when she half-rose, becoming a shrill high command as she pointed her gold staff directly at Osip and Jily.

'Guards, seize those two. They are traitors!'

Two more of the black-and-red uniformed guards appeared from behind and grabbed them. Queen Veka was standing now, and she pointed the staff again like a witch's wand of death.

'Off with their heads!'

14 Under the axe-blade

Jily froze, incredulous for a moment. Then two
things flashed through her mind. The power surge
is affecting this dream-clip as well – and it was time
to get out of here. She grabbed for the control on
her wrist but her arms were wrenched painfully back
by the guard. Queen Veka came sweeping up the
room, her gaudy flock of courtiers scattering before
her. Her eyes were icy cold and she spoke from a
haughty distance, as though addressing strangers.

'Take them out!'

'Veka, this is not the Tudor Age, the court of
Queen Elizabeth—' That was Osip and a guard
turned, back-handing him hard across the face.

'Speak not to Her Majesty, dog!'

'Veka—'

And another hard hand smashed in Jily's mouth,
cutting her off the same way. On the floor, an
embroidered skirt hem swished the control away
and a jewelled shoe kicked it further. She glimpsed
Veka's eyes blazing with malicious triumph as the
guards dragged her out.

They were pulled outside into a stone-flagged,
high-walled courtyard. Oh hell, Veka's really paying
us back, thought Jily; she's on a power trip. Does she
know those blows hurt us – does she care? The court
was swarming round them, the short stocky men in
their bright tunics and armour, the women in their
sweeping gowns and high wigs. Each held a fan to her

face and Jily thought of Angharad's fingernails. They were in the centre of the courtyard now, before a low wooden platform. It was covered with straw and set in the middle was a big slab of wood with a U-shaped notch in the top. The execution block!

'Osip . . .'

'We'll be all right—' He was only half-conscious and slumped as a guard hit him again. Now they were binding her hands behind her back with tight leather straps. Veka's shrill voice cut through the babble round them.

'The girl first!'

Jily was being dragged up the steps on to the platform. She opened her mouth to try one last time and twisted her head as she saw the blow coming. She kicked out and felt her foot connect. Then a fist thumped into her stomach and she was flung to her knees, half-winded and gasping. A man was stepping up before her. He was clad in greasy black clothes with a black hood over his face, and tying on a leather apron like a butcher getting ready to cut meat. He picked up a long-bladed axe whose sharp edge glinted in the sunlight.

'Let it begin!' came Veka's delighted tones.

It's happening, thought Jily, with a curious, horrible sense of unreality. She was kneeling on the matted straw and the man in black was ripping her collar away and baring her neck. Beyond the block was a tattered, black-stained wicker basket.

Her knees hurt against the cracked boards of the scaffold; she went rigid with horror as the man stepped back and the shadow of his axe-swing began travelling back over the straw. She tried to speak once more but a hand pushed her head down and her chin banged painfully against the sharp edge of the block. She choked on the stench of the filthy straw, the block cold against her throat and the taste of blood in her mouth. The stink of straw was too much and she shut her eyes. That's the last thing I'll ever smell, she thought. Something jarred and shook her from top to toe, but her head was still on her shoulders as she spun round and the stinking straw changed into fresh green grass, flowers and brown earth.

Jily was still kneeling, but the tight cords binding her wrists had disappeared. She brought her hands round to the front and opened her eyes into the sunlight and natural beauty of the Venusian Cretaceous Age. Osip was standing beside her and he put out a shaky hand to help Jily up. Her mouth still hurt.

'I hope that teaches you both a lesson,' came a voice behind them.

Veka was standing behind them, still clad in her Elizabethan costume, hands on hips, Jily's control clipped to the ornate lace of one sleeve. She was a bizarre picture against the landscape, but still looked dignified, as a queen should. Before Jily spoke, she wiped a small dribble of blood from her mouth and Veka's eyes widened with astonishment.

'You're not supposed to bleed.'

'Thanks for telling us,' said Osip. He held up a hand and Veka winced at the sight of his skinned knuckles.

'What happened?' she whispered.

'Have a look around you, Queen Veka,' said Jily angrily.

Veka did. It was as though she hadn't noticed before where she was. Now, all at once she did look out of place and her costume became grotesque and clumsy. 'What sort of dream-clip is this? Why am I still wearing these? And why didn't we zap out?'

'This dream-clip has been overtaken by real events that happened on Venus a few million years ago,' interrupted Osip. 'And when it overlaps into other dream-clips, it makes them real.'

Now Veka was looking stupid and flustered in her huge pearl-embroidered gown and the high red wig. She pulled the wig off and threw it into a yellow-flowered bush.

'Where are we?' Veka shook out her red hair.

'Venusian dinosaur age,' said Osip. 'Watch out for the deinos—'

'They're nearly as bad as your executioner.' Jily couldn't make herself speak as calmly as Osip. She could still smell that straw and see the backward shadow of the axe-swing.

Veka looked at her and gave a titter. It was only the twang of high-strung nerves, but it was too much for Jily. She put her head down and charged, butting into Veka's skirt-folds and stomach. They crashed over together, Veka's legs kicking up under the long skirt.

'Hey, stop it!' shouted Osip.

Jily was in no mood to stop it and neither was Veka. This had been coming too long for both of them. They rolled over, punching and slapping and trying to grab each other round the neck. Osip tried twice to separate them. The first time Veka kicked him and the second time Jily elbowed his stomach. Then they rolled over again and a stink worse than all of Tudor England hit them both at the same time. They sat up, coughing and choking and scrambled to their feet.

'Satisfied?' Osip was rubbing his stomach but trying to grin at the same time.

Jily and Veka had rolled into the pile of ripe brakky droppings. Veka had collected most of it, all over her priceless gown and face. She rubbed one jewelled sleeve down her cheek and glared angrily, ripping apart the bodice strings and smearing the gown with more sticky brown patches as she tried to pull it off. Osip, then Jily, silently took hold of a sleeve each and dragged the huge thing over her head. Veka collapsed – and sat down in the same pile of dung again. Jily and Osip pulled her up again and this time their silence spoke louder than words. Jily looked at the neat imprint made by Veka's bottom; maybe one day that would appear in the fossil record too.

Underneath, Veka had on a sleep-robe and she began cleaning herself with a handful of grass. 'What the hell have you two managed to do?' she scowled.

'We—'

A loud honking squawk interrupted them and a shadow passed overhead. A huge version of the pterodactyls, tan-coloured and with a long red crest and a wingspan of some ten metres, was gliding majestically, angling its line of flight, down the river. There was puzzled terror on Veka's face now; for the first time, Jily felt sorry for her.

'We'd better do some explaining,' she said.

'You've got mindspread too,' said Jily to Veka. 'That made the reality of the dream-caps even more powerful. Without being aware, you were controlling it. You still are.'

They had walked down to the river and sat by the bank. As she listened, Veka pulled off her rings.

135

They formed a small glittering pile at her feet and she picked them up, one by one, and threw them into the steel-blue water.

'So these aren't real?' She took off her long diamond and pearl earrings and cupped them in her hands, letting the sunlight flash and sparkle over the jewels. 'They seem real enough.'

'Free-formed like the remote control. The Venusian energy is charging our virtual reality helmets and making them real. But only inside our heads.'

'Then how can we be hurt?'

'Our minds will tell our bodies we're hurt and our bodies will respond,' Osip said. 'Like hypnosis or auto-suggestion.'

Veka looked at him and threw the earrings into the river, one after the other. The second time, a wide-mouthed, blue-speckled fish rose and snapped at the earring as though it was a juicy, glittering worm.

'Then you've landed us in something very heavy.'

'This was all waiting to happen,' said Jily. She looked up at the pale comet outlined in the blue sky. It was larger now.

'Then we have to tell Corp.'

There was a note in Veka's voice, though, that Jily and Osip both picked up on. Whatever her loyalties to Corp, she was feeling the magic sunlit warmth of all this strange reality, and she rubbed her face uncertainly. A large butterfly perched on her red hair like a floppy yellow bow.

'We think Corp knows,' said Osip. 'At least some of this.'

'Prove it.' The old challenge was back in Veka's voice.

'They know,' said Jily. And there was a note in her voice now that made both Veka and Osip look at her. She could feel something hurting in each word she spoke. 'They know because a friend of mine was on Purple Zero before me. His name was Andi and he had mindspread like me. He was one of those first JOKS to come to Venus.'

There was silence. Jily's eyes were misting as though that thick Tudor glass was over them, but she went on. Now the pain kept tangling the words.

'Andi had mindspread too, because of doomfire. It must have affected him the way it did me. Andi never kept secrets. He would have told Corp – or Parthenope. He would've been too excited not to.' The tears were trickling down her cheeks now, but she didn't care. 'Don't you all see? There was no rockfall. Nothing would get them all together like that. They came here exploring . . .'

'And never left . . .' whispered Osip.

'Corp must have seen what happened – whatever happened to their bodies as their minds were locked under the dream-caps. So they made it all look like an accident. I was the closest to Andi so I replaced my friend.'

'To see if the same thing would happen . . .' came Osip's voice, but Jily didn't answer. She had her hands over her face and hot tears swimming over her fingers. She felt someone kneel beside her. Not now, Osip, she wanted to say, but it was Veka who spoke and put her arms round Jily.

'Shouldn't we ask Corp then?' Her voice was so gentle that Jily's tears became stronger. 'At least . . .'

She broke off and jumped to her feet. Jily opened her eyes, tears forgotten as a distant wailing sound grew louder and louder. As though an unseen creature was howling as it stalked them for the kill. Then Osip shouted.

'The base alarm – coming through our dream-caps! Jily—'

Jily was already on her feet and reaching for the sleeve-remote. She blinked hard and pressed the button and—

She was looking at the cubicle wall as the dream-cap lifted. Around them was the horrible deafening wail of the siren, still growing in intensity like hard slamming wave beats as they ran through to the control area. Angharad was there, pacing up and down behind the screen like a cat in a cage. She saw them and began to speak. Then the siren cut and they plainly heard her words, breathless, high-pitched, very unlike her usual smooth composure.

'Where've you been?'

And there was something wrong with the screen too. Normally it was so real they could almost step into it. Today it was misted and flat and forked lines cut sharply through like electronic scissors.

'What's the matter?' gasped Osip.

Now Herilbert had appeared. 'You must keep calm, children. We'll help as much as we can.'

'What's *wrong*?' yelled Veka.

Angharad hesitated, suddenly at a loss for words. 'There seems to be undefined interference in the tel-sparks.' More scissor-lines split her and Herilbert into a sharp-angled jigsaw. 'It seems to be coming from an unidentified space-craft orbiting Venus on an entry—'

The scissor-lines flicked together and the screen went dead. 'Unidentified spacecraft?' said Veka.

'Probably just Nel—' then she stopped. Too stupid – Corp would know the difference. Osip went quickly to the control screens and punched in the surface code. The astrodome monitor zapped into sharp clarity.

Only for seconds, but long enough to see the spaceship squatting itself down on three stubby fins; a flat bug-eyed toad, which seemed to ignore the terrible blasting heat-storms around it. Jily had seen something like that before and knew with a heavy stomach-bounce what she was looking at.

An alien spaceship landing on the surface of Venus.

15   Aliens in the base

'There are no such things as Betels,' whispered
Veka as though reading the words from a prepared
Corp statement. 'Betels do not exist, they are a
rumour—'

She stopped speaking as though someone had cut
a switch and stood looking at the blank screen. Osip
had gone over and was running his fingers over the
keyboard. 'Communication cut,' he said. 'Everything
is zapped.'

Jily stood there too. She knew how Veka was
feeling. There was a tingling, rigid feeling in her body
because once again on Purple Zero, the impossible
was happening. Aliens from somewhere in the universe were outside and soon they would be coming
in. She made herself open her mouth and speak.

'We have to do something.'

'Do something?' Osip looked round from the blank
screen. 'We haven't got a gun between us. We don't
know what those things can do—'

'Yes!' Veka's words snapped out, sharpened with
an edge of panic. 'We have to do something, defend
Corp property, use the laser drills, anything!'

'They might not want to hurt us,' said Osip.

'We can't just wait and find out,' said Jily.

Osip shut his eyes a moment. Jily knew that sign
now – he was thinking hard and fast. And he was
just as scared as them, but trying not to show it.
'All right, Jily, get up in the astrodome and see what

they're doing.' Jily gave him a tight smile to show he wasn't alone, and headed for the stairs.

Outside, the red wind-storm seemed to have died. The alien spaceship was settled, engines shut off and an airlock opening in the side. A round, four-wheeled vehicle came out. At least we know they've invented the wheel, thought Jily, then couldn't believe she was thinking crazy little things like that. The vehicle was like a long tube and it trundled slowly over the uneven orange-red surface. She crouched, looking just over the top, and heard Osip whisper below.

'What's happening?'

'They're sending something across.' Jily scrambled back down the stairs. 'Osip, I'm scared.'

'So am I.' He tried to grin.

'We have to fight them,' came Veka's voice. She was over by the rack of laser drills, testing how long she could make the cutting flame. 'We have to show them that humans don't go down easily.'

The hands that were adjusting the cutting flame were shaking, though. Jily knew that Veka was as scared as they were and trying – like them – to keep it tightly stoppered. And she liked Veka more for that.

'We can't fight them,' said Osip. 'Maybe we can hide somewhere.'

'Hide!' flashed Veka.

'Yes! Corp doesn't need dead heroes – and we have to tell Earth about the Betels,' shouted Jily.

'So where do we hide?' said Veka.

She knew the answer as well as they did. There was nowhere. Down here in the mining chamber, up in the control area, or the sleeping quarters, there was nowhere to hide one person, let alone three; even to alien eyes that perhaps looked on a different light or colour wavelength. And overhead came a loud clanking sound, echoing from the entry lock into the mining chamber. The aliens were opening the lock and would soon be down the tunnel and into the base. And there they would find three kids alone, their Copies defunct, no weapons and communication cut with Earth and Corp. The clanking sound echoed again and Jily screwed her eyes shut as she thought hard. The chamber, the control area, the sleeping quarters, their dream-caps – and like the pattern on Angharad's fingernails, her mind level shifted and a new pattern flashed into sharp focus.

There *was* somewhere to hide!

'Somewhere!' she yelled, echoing the word in her mind. 'Somewhere they may not think of looking for us. But we'll have to move quickly! Follow me.'

They did move, very quickly, but were only just in place when the airlock door unsealed itself with a loud thudding click. Jily was in her place; she could see nothing of Osip or Veka and made herself go rigid. But nothing happened. Then more nothing and even more, for a very long time. Jily's own breathing was sounding too loud in her ears and she tried to suck it down into a gentle hiss. She could still hear nothing. Were the aliens somehow floating without sound – or had they already seen their hiding-place with cruel inhuman eyes?

Then a sudden clattering sound nearly made her jump. Jily stilled herself – any movement would be fatal! She could see through a narrow slit, just a section of the stairs that led down to the ice-tunnel and a pair of metal-booted feet clanked into view.

At least they've got legs like us, she thought, aware her breathing was loud again. Slowly, through her narrow slot, the rest of the thing came into view. First she saw the long ribbed legs of steel, then a shimmering metal garment that covered the body and a conical sharp-pointed helmet with an all-round crystal eye-mask. She nearly jumped again as the thing stopped and a sibilant voice whispered in the darkness.

'Earth children?'

The words were clipped and jumbled as though their syllables were patched together by an audio computer but underlaid with a harsh, deadly note of menace. Jily had such a sudden desire to answer that she bit her teeth into her tongue and tasted blood. She was hot, the sweat trickled down her face and her body ached.

'Children?'

She had the sudden, silly desire to answer again and this time bit her tongue harder, tasting more blood. She could not see Osip or Veka, but they only had to make one movement or sound to give them all away. Oh, don't let them think of looking for us here, she prayed. Then the thing moved on as another pair of clanging footsteps began to follow the first. Another pair of metal-ribbed legs and a shimmering, metal tunic hem came into view.

'Nobody – here?' asked a second clipped computer-patched voice.

'Get – the – doomfire,' croaked the first voice.

Doomfire! So even the aliens knew about it. Jily couldn't move and a cramp was starting in her leg. Once they had fought wars on Earth over oil, she thought; maybe that's what the first interstellar war will be about – with us caught in the crossfire. The cramp was getting worse, biting like strong teeth into her leg; Jily felt a wave of panic that threatened to make her shiver, shake, stretch her body. She was going to move – she let a silent scream grow louder in her head. Then, with a loud tuning buzz, she felt Osip's presence and heard his voice. 'I can feel you Jily. I know it's tough. Don't move!'

Then something else, as though her mind had slipped another wavelength and darkness, curious and probing, closed around. An alien mind! Jily shut herself off frantically, trying not to move as she heard the footsteps clanging. Had the Betels sensed something? Then the footsteps went off down the ice-tunnel and as much as she dared, Jily relaxed. She didn't dare try and contact Osip again.

One pair of footsteps clanged back up the stairs, then came down again. Then both pairs, shuffling as though holding something heavy between them, up the stairs and whispering too low for her to hear. Then both pairs came down again – then up, and down again. The clanging sound began to din inside Jily's head with a dull, alien pounding and still she could not move. The sweat ran down her face and the cramp nipped its way up her legs. More clanging steps and one of those computer-patched voices – the first – spoke again.

'Leave – exit – airlock—'

Leave by the airlock? Jily scarcely dared breathe with hope, but it seemed they were going. The footsteps were clanging upstairs again, more long moments, then suddenly the cramp bit her hard and she flinched, moving. Things clattered loudly round

145

her as she sat up and she heard Veka's low cry of
dismay.

'That's done it.'

For another moment, there was no noise, then
they all heard the sudden click-thud of the closing
airlock door in the distance. The aliens had gone.
They helped each other stand. Osip pushed back her
visor and then his own.

'I think they've gone.'

Veka was standing. Behind her, the reinforcing
rods that fitted into the Copies' arms and legs clattered down from where she had stacked them. She
undid the front section of her Copy helmet and pulled
it off, shaking out her red hair with a sigh of relief.

'I'll check,' she said, and still clad in the metal-
skinned body, arms and legs, she clumped heavily
over and up the stairs.

Osip was pulling his own Copy head off. He was
still pale, but grinned. 'Good one, Jily.'

Jily grinned back. 'It was brilliant,' she said
modestly.

Copies were made to look humanoid, but inside
they were circuits and flexible rods, operated from
the power-pack on the back. They could be disman-
tled and literally boxed up. It had been simple to pull
out circuits, disconnect the rods and slip themselves
into the hollow, flexible, alloy skin, and clip the
copy-head over their own. Then, to lie down – just
in time – like disconnected Copies, as the first alien
footsteps had clanged through Purple Zero. Osip
helped her pull off the long stocking-legs and she
helped him, still fighting that silly need to giggle.
The best hiding-places were the most obvious. Veka
came back down the stairs.

'Gone,' she said, pulling her own Copy arms off.

'Check the astrodome, Jily,' said Osip. He went over to help Veka.

Above, a dust-storm had started again, whipping round the spaceship and buffeting the tube-vehicle as it trundled to the opening airlock.

'Taking off again, I think,' she called.

The control room and sleeping quarters were the same. Nothing had been touched. The screen was blank and Osip fiddled with the controls a moment, then shrugged despairingly.

'Everything's dead,' he said.

'How long before we get communication back?' said Veka.

'Depends on Earth.' Osip shrugged again. 'If the tel-sparks have been blown, a long time.'

'Nel will be back soon,' said Jily, but she ended on an uncertain note because the same thought occurred to all three. Maybe the Betels had got Nel too.

'Earth-children!' burst out Veka suddenly. 'That's what they called out! They were expecting someone.'

'And doomfire,' said Jily.

'They must have picked up Gobnait's transmission,' said Osip. 'Anyway, they didn't find us.'

'Thanks to Jily,' said Veka stiffly, with the barest hint of a smile.

'They came for the doomfire,' said Jily. She tried to smile back, but the reaction was setting in. Butterflies were galloping in her stomach and a headache was starting.

'Let's see how much they took,' said Osip. 'Veka, stay by the control screen. If something comes through, yell.' She nodded and Jily followed him

147

down. At the bottom, he put his arms round her. 'You were great, Jily.'

'Take more than Betels to stop us, won't it?' Jily smiled back, but those butterflies were still galloping round her stomach and Osip sensed the strain. He nodded, sure, and headed for the ice-tunnel.

'They spent a long time down here, just to get a sample,' said Jily. And she felt a sudden tingle of unease.

'When we had jungles on Earth, explorers used to go into them to collect specimens,' said Osip. His voice echoed round the close glimmering walls. 'Maybe that's all the Betels were doing.'

'Maybe,' said Jily.

But that feeling of unease was crowding in as though the glimmering ice-walls were telegraphing a message of warning through her. They turned the corner and reached the ice-wall, shining and glowing that beautiful silvery blue colour. On the ground lay one of their laser drills and a neat triangular section of doomfire had been removed. But they ignored those things and just stared ahead.

Jily was remembering the first rumours about Betels. A freighter had gone missing; it was a mining shuttle, so that must be where the Betels got these from, she thought: 'alot'. It's used to blow asteroids apart for their minerals. Kana and Dar had talked about alot. The stuff came in long, slim, black cylinders and one was enough to blow a normal-sized asteroid apart.

And there were dozens of the long black cylinders packed round the ice-face. All were red-tipped and in the tip, a little detonating light flashed, winking at Osip and Jily like evil green eyes. No wonder the

148

aliens had taken so long, thought Jily. They were busy packing all this into place.

Enough explosive to blow Purple Zero from the face of Venus.

16   *Journey up to Hell*

Jily and Osip took a backward step at the same
time. They heard Veka yell, demanding to know
what they had found, but didn't answer. Osip took
a deep swallowing breath before he spoke.

'Let's get them up the chute.'

Jily caught his arm. 'My guardians were miners.
That stuff will explode when the heat hits it. The
first one will jam the chute.'

'Can we move some? Lessen the impact?'

'The detonation lights are on. They'll explode
when we touch them.' Everything Jily had heard
came zipping into her mind like data on-screen. 'It
needs a master detonator . . .'

She was trying to remember and shut her eyes the
way Osip did when he was thinking. Kana had taken
her out in one of the giant Gobblers once to watch an
auto-probe planting explosive to expose magnesium.
What had Kana shouted over the loud roar of the
engine?

'. . . Master detonator, a remote control, somewhere.'

'On the spaceship?' said Osip.

There was a clatter of feet as Veka came running
up and stopped behind them. Jily shut her eyes
again, still remembering. 'They'd have to be too
high when this lot goes up. A remote signal might
not get through the clouds—' Jily stopped and felt
her insides blend madly as the green eyes winked

151

gleefully at them. We're going to blow you all to atoms, said those evil winks, and let Venus sizzle what is left.

Veka was white as death, her mouth open. She took a backward step just as they had done, but a resolute glint came into her green eyes. 'So what do we do?'

'Check the spaceship,' said Osip. He meant Jily, but Veka was off down the tunnel. Jily and Osip took another scared look and fled after her.

The three of them were a tight squeeze in the astrodome, each trying to look over the other.

Jily had never felt more like a scared kid than now, squeezed between Osip and Veka, looking through the iron-glass of the astrodome. The Betel spaceship was still there, but the airlock had closed and there were clouds of red dust round the massive engines.

Osip muttered something and ducked back down the stairs. Veka followed. Jily stayed there, watching as the red dust clouds grew thicker, blotting the spaceship from sight. It's getting up power to thrust itself away from Venus gravity, she thought. It'll go up and just before cloud-cover, it'll send a signal. We've got ten minutes, maybe fifteen – how long *have* we got?

In the control room, Osip was flipping pictures through one of the screens. 'Have we got control back?' Jily asked as she came up.

'No. The base monitors are working, though, and I'm trying to find the detonation relay.' He flipped more pictures from the monitor cameras set outside to check for damage or danger. The red hell of Venus flared outside the massive entry doors, then the picture cut to an inside half-light.

'Where's that?' whispered Veka.

'Inside the entry tunnel.' The light was showing a pair of massive steel rails that would have locked to the underside of Nel's shuttle. Slowly Osip worked the monitor picture down.

Then Jily shouted. 'There!' She pointed. Inside the entry tunnel at the end, a small heavy circular plate was attached to the entry airlock door. A mini-screen digital readout flashed in the middle of it. 'They won't need a relay signal,' breathed Jily. 'That's an automatic timer and it's been pre-set.'

'Then let's get to it!' Veka made to move and Jily grabbed her arm.

'No! It's automatic, fixed against the airlock with magnetic clips!' She watched as Osip brought up the picture in bigger images. 'If we open this side and it falls—'

'It'll fuse?' said Osip, looking round.

'We have to take that chance!' yelled Veka.

'We can't.'

Osip had enhanced the picture until it filled the screen. Beside the circular timer, circuits and wires were hanging out of an open slot.

'I think they fused the lock and fixed the circuits to the timer for power.' Osip was trying to speak calmly. 'If we open that door we'll send a power surge through the detonator.'

'Nothing then.' Veka's voice was flat and she took a step back. 'We just wait for it to blow.' Her hands clenched and unclenched, she opened and shut her mouth and gave a little head-shake of terror. She didn't speak and somehow that made it worse for Jily. Veka was a girl who never gave up – and she was giving up now.

'Twenty minutes,' said Osip. He had enhanced the picture until the timer itself filled the screen, the digital numbers flicking down even as he spoke. This was the end!

'The other exit is the rubbish chute,' said Osip wryly.

The rubbish chute. A grid pattern of the base was forming in Jily's mind. The mining chamber, the chute and the big entry doors you could see when standing in the astrodome. And something else, something outside the astrodome that should have been crushed by the Venus gravity.

'We could get out of the chute, over to the entry doors and down through the tunnel.' Jily spoke slowly as though the words were printing themselves inside her mind.

'Out of the chute?' Veka was incredulous. 'And get squashed flat then burned alive?'

'We might not get crushed,' said Jily. Osip was registering, looking at her. 'The silver-ice we ejected is pure energy and somehow makes its own forcefield when it melts – pushing back the gravity.'

'We'd be roasted alive by the heat!' shouted Veka.

'Not if we wore a Copy suit.' Even Osip hadn't registered on that one and Veka just gaped at her. 'They'd keep the heat out.' The other two were just looking at her and on-screen, the digits flickered down. Eighteen minutes already. Jily's voice rose to a shout. 'Androids like these built this base, so their alloy skins must be heat resistant.'

'For how long?' said Osip.

Jily looked at the flickering digitals again. 'I think we're going to find out the hard way,' she said.

*   *   *

The arms, legs and body tunic of the Copies sealed to each other with a stuff like super-Velcro. Jily pulled on the thick gloved hands and pressed them tight to the wrist-bands. She felt as though a second thick skin had been glued on to her body. Beside her, Veka's red hair tumbled on brass-covered shoulders and she bunched it up behind to push under the Copy helmet Osip was fitting over her head.

Then he fitted Jily's helmet. She had time to notice it was lined with that purple insulation stuff. But how many Copies had melted before the base was built? How long would it keep out the fire-storm heat of Venus? Osip shut the neck lock tight. He made to speak, but there were tears in his eyes and they were prickling at the corners of hers. Then he snapped down the visor mask and she could only glimpse his face through the narrow slit that normally let in sunlight for solar energy.

'Ready?' he said.

Jily mumbled something back and beside her, Veka echoed it. The Copy back-pack had been stripped and a little emergency air-tank fitted with a tube through the Copy skin to the helmet and their mouths. Enough air for ten minutes, if the fire-storms let them live that long.

There was room in the chute for one person to sit huddled. The door slammed shut and Jily knew what a piece of rubbish felt like as she whizzed up to the surface, spun round and ejected with a blast of compressed air on to the surface of Venus.

She staggered to her knees. The chute had been close and hot, but the blast of heat here hit like a tempest, a screaming live inferno that was already stabbing red-hot fingers through every part of her body. The gravity pressed a crushing red hand down, but she could just stand upright as the chute slammed again and Veka came tumbling out. Jily was hot, but the Copy skin seemed to be deflecting most of the heat. She pulled Veka up and pointed to the low slitted entrance ahead half-hidden by the storming orange-red dust.

They turned towards it. Round them, through their thick helmets, came a wild inhuman howling, growing stronger. Another, even more powerful storm was sweeping up on red-hot feet. Jily sucked air as the blast hit her and pointed again as she linked arms with Veka and staggered towards the entrance. She was hot now, the sweat running off her but drying as the heat scorched through her body. Even the metal nozzle of her air tube was hot in her mouth and her lips were burning. The pressure was getting heavier and she felt her knees begin to buckle. We must be getting outside the forcefield of energy, she thought, because the gravity is hitting us. Beside her, Veka stumbled; they were still metres short. She pulled Veka up, but her own metal-booted foot hit an uneven edge of rock. Twisting pain stabbed up from her ankle and she fell heavily.

Jily tried to get up, but the same sharp pain stabbed through her ankle. Twisted, she thought, can't move. Veka had gone on to the hatch. I would have too, thought Jily – the precious minutes are slipping by. The heat force-blasted on to her body and she felt herself slipping down, the hard hot surface of Venus against her metal-skinned body. Sorry, Osip, but one of us will get through . . .

Then something pushed against Jily and a pair of glowing metal arms slid round her. Veka was standing there like a red-hot metal statue. She slipped Jily's arm round her shoulder and pulled her up. Jily came back alive, choking back a scream of agony as sharp pain shot through her ankle.

Veka was dragging her along but her own feet stumbled on the uneven red-hot surface. Now the impossible heat was penetrating through Jily's body. 'Leave me, get inside,' her voice screamed and deafened inside the hollow Copy head, but she knew Veka could not hear her. Ahead of them, a black line was appearing. It was Osip, back underground at the monitor, operating the controls. The black line grew wider and Veka thumped against her. One last effort, the movement said, but now the gravity was pushing hard. They were nearly out of the forcefield and the pressure was hitting them, the heat flowing over like a solid molten wave. Three steps, each sending a worse stab of agony up her ankle as the gravity pressed harder. Jily collapsed against the opening door and Veka pushed her through.

She was hot, so hot that she couldn't move. Veka's glowing hands were holding her tightly, dragging her as the doors slid shut and straight away a half-darkness closed round them. Veka was on her knees and falling forward on her face, her last strength gone. Jily tried to get up and a voice boomed inside the heat and half-light.

'Jily!'

Osip, on the base intercom, was shouting to her. The glowing on her alloy-skin had faded a little; she could still hear Osip shouting and got to her knees. The two tunnel rails stretched ahead and down and Jily slid forward like a swimmer in deep water on to one of the rails. She held tight, feeling the hot,

157

smooth metal rub against her alloy-skin as she slid down, faster and faster, towards the bottom and the airlock door where the digital timer must be flicking out their last moments.

The rails inclined more steeply and Jily clung tight, aware she was going faster. Then quite suddenly she shot off the end and crashed up against the wall, a fresh wave of pain banging through her head, making her black out.

'Jily, get up!'

What was Osip shouting about now? Everything was black and drifting round her; nothing mattered and funny disconnected thoughts floated in her mind. Her head hurt, like the time she tumbled over an exercise machine in the Moonbase gym. Kana had fussed over her in the nice way she did and she hadn't sent Kana that post-spark either.

'Jily – thirty seconds!'

Osip's voice again. Thirty what? Nothing mattered – she wanted to get that post-spark and send it to Kana; there was one in her bag under the bed and she rolled over. She heard Osip again. Was it time to get up and start work? She sat up. A sudden piercing stab went through her foot and she screamed as Osip's voice resounded round her.

'Jily! Ten seconds!'

The pain shocked her back like a dazzling burst of doomfire. Jily pushed up her visor. The timer was in front and she took a step forward, nearly collapsing on her bad ankle.

'Five seconds!'

She took a deep breath, three more steps – each time the pain worse than before – and dived forward. Ahead the red digits were flickering down and showed 'one' as her metalfingered hand hit the red cut-off button over the timer. The digital readout changed to 'O', then the screen went blank and Jily waited just a moment to know that Purple Zero wasn't exploding before a thick darkness spun her helplessly round and, in slow motion, the base floor came up and hit her.

Then the darkness lifted a little and she could feel hot air on her face. She blinked and opened her eyes against the hissing stream. Veka was kneeling beside her, playing her air nozzle over Jily's face.

'Are you all right?' she said, as gently as the time Jily had talked about Andi – a million years ago in another time, it seemed. Veka threw down the air-tank and helped her sit upright against the tunnel wall.

'Yes,' she nodded. She could hear air being pumped into the tunnel and a sigh that didn't come from Veka; she realised it was Osip on the intercom. It was a sigh of relief and Veka nearly smiled.

'You saved us Jily,' came Osip's voice. 'You were both wonderful.'

'Thanks for coming back,' whispered Jily.

Veka blinked with a quick press of her lips. 'All right,' she said, in a defensive and hurried way. 'Let's get that circuit repaired.'

'Detonator lights are out on the alot cylinders,' came Osip's voice. 'Can we move them now?'

'No.' Jily was feeling dizzy and her ankle still hurt badly. 'We should wait for Nel.'

She wanted to faint again. And it was odd saying that name, because a strong image leaped so quickly in her mind. The big black-clad woman with her crooked cynical grin and braid of black hair. Her head spun and the Nel-image came again, that harsh voice seeming to boom round the tunnel. She blinked again and shook her aching head to clear it, then became aware Veka was looking round. And the loud, harsh voice echoed again.

'Come on, wake up you bloody JOKs!'

Nel's angry voice was all round them on the intercom. And they could hear Osip, frantically trying to raise her at the controls.

'I can't reach her. We can't transmit!'

'All right, I'm overriding,' snapped the harsh voice.

'Osip, can you raise her?' shouted Veka.

'Too late.' His voice was despairing. 'She's got control and I don't know the codes to break it.'

Jily felt dizzy again and light-headed. There was an old Earth expression Kana sometimes used, 'Out of the frying pan into the fire.' There were no frying pans any more, or open fires. But there would be fiery heat from the shuttle's exhaust when Nel docked and even if they weren't roasted alive, the shuttle's own weight sliding down the rails would crush them against the back wall quicker than Venus' gravity. Nel's voice crackled again, loud and impatient.

'Coming in.'

17   Moon-fall into nightmare

Veka yelled and began tugging her metal glove hands off. 'There's half an hour's work on these circuits,' she shouted. 'How long have we got?'

'Nel's last run-up took ten minutes,' came Osip's voice.

'Then I'd better work fast.' Veka threw her last glove hand at the wall and Jily noticed her fingers tremble as she grabbed the circuit leads. She stood up, her head buzzing, her ankle still sending knife stabs up her leg. She took a step over and Veka waved her back. 'I can work faster alone.'

'Osip, keep trying!' Jily yelled.

'I am, but I can't break the override!' She could feel the desperation in her voice, then a sudden snap of hope. 'Wait—' He broke off and Jily could see those big graceful hands on the keyboard, the tense tight-lipped look on his face. He sounded cool enough. I'd be screaming if I was him, she thought—'No. I got her Copy wavelength but that's blocked, too.'

Another sharp pain went up Jily's ankle and she nearly cried out. Then something driven by the pain, as sharp and strong, flashed into her mind. 'Osip, telepathy. Maybe I can make my mind contact her!'

Veka darted an incredulous glance. They hadn't told her about Jily's mind powers. Osip's voice came back, thinking hard as he spoke. 'When you were stressed out, without thinking—' He stopped for a

161

moment. Jily's ankle made her slip and she banged her head against the wall. The pain clicked something else in her mind, something that hurt like contact points from a helmet.

'The Copy!'

Veka swung round. 'What?'

'Yes!' Osip's excited shout echoed round them. 'Jily, put on the helmet and I'll patch their wavelength to the contact points. Then concentrate!'

Jily fitted the helmet on as Osip told Veka what was happening. And over Veka's 'this is crazy' reaction, she clipped it into place and felt the contact points dig into her head. Nel spoke again as she made to lower the visor.

'Five minutes. If you JOKs are OK and listening, keep away from the controls – and you'd better have a good story.'

Behind Veka, the circuits dangled loose. She shook her head again and muttered. 'Try it.'

Jily lowered the visor and snapped it shut. She jammed the helmet down hard and felt the terminal signal buzzing through the points. She still didn't have any real idea how this worked or how the doomfire boosted her. Got to be with Nel, she thought, and she tried to set a visual image of the control cabin in her mind. Nel in one chair, the Pilot-Copy in the other. No, that wasn't right – she had to be in the copy chair. A brass-skinned Copy with that distinctive little crest down its head. She blinked her eyes open, but through the narrow slit she could see Veka, her back turned, working frantically at the circuits. And Nel's voice again, black as death.

'Two minutes!'

Then the airlock doors would open! Jily shut her eyes and tried hard. But the suit felt heavy. There were painful little throbs from the contact points against her head and an odd disjointed feeling flowed over her as though she was about to faint again. And to mock her futile efforts, Nel's voice again, as harsh and loud as ever.

'One minute. Opening airlock.'

Jily tried to concentrate, but there was just that queer floating feeling again. Then suddenly she realised Nel's voice hadn't echoed the last time she spoke. She opened her eyes and through the thick visor slit, she saw controls and felt her metal body rigid in the chair. And as if in slow motion, like a horrible dream, Nel's black-gloved hand was going out to the console, about to press a button. And she knew – *knew* it would open the lock. There was that last unreal moment before her own body-awareness was flooding through the Copy body, her own metal glove hand going out. There was no sense of feeling, just a sense of control as her metal fingers tightly grabbed the black-sleeved arm.

'No – we're in the entry tunnel, me and Veka. I'm Jily!'

Her voice was booming loudly in the Copy head. Nel had frozen. Utter shock stamped itself on her crooked face for a moment, but with the hair-trigger reactions of a good pilot she was already recovering. She tore her arm free and jerked the control stick back. The shuttle reared up into the scarlet teeth of another fire-storm, heading for the thick clouds. 'How are you voice-linking into my Copy?' she said, the same flat harsh tone in her voice.

'I'm not. My mind's in here somehow.'

'Purple Zero, I'm going into a holding pattern above cloud-cover,' snapped Nel. She sat there, her mouth in that rat-trap line, intent on the controls as Jily tried to explain. The cloud cover was close around them, then they broke free and through the Copy's visor slit, Jily felt the sharp dazzle of sunlight. Nel set the controls on automatic and turned to look at Jily.

'I'm going to open your visor and look inside.' Her crooked smile was back in place. 'Sit still.'

Her hand reached out past the visor and Jily swung her metal arm up, incredibly light and fast, knocking Nel's fingers from her brass neck.

'Don't try it.'

Nel had been reaching for the cut-off switch at the back of the helmet. She glared and stood up, towering like a grim monster over Jily. 'Listen, you—'

Jily put out a hand, just to stop Nel getting too close. She meant it to be a gentle stopping movement but Nel went staggering back, collapsing over her chair and her booted legs kicking in the air.

'Sorry, Nel. I don't know my own strength.'

Nel recovered and stood up, rubbing her head. For the first time, she looked puzzled and uncertain – but still not scared. 'It really is you, not just my Copy crossing wave-bands. How the hell did you do that?'

The sunlight dazzled Jily's visor again and she felt very weak, her control slipping. That stabbing pain was starting again. 'Never mind that. Give Osip the codes. He'll tell you.'

'Anything to oblige.' Nel spoke quickly as the shuttle skimmed over the thick cloud-cover. They heard Osip reply and Nel looked at Jily again, the

164

crooked smile back firmly in place. 'Now get out of my Copy. I need it.'

'OK.' Jily paused a moment – she could feel her control slipping away. There was something else, something she'd nearly forgotten. 'Watch out for Betels. They were in the base—'

Nel's crooked smile slipped and her eyes went wide. But two wave-bands were separating in Jily's head; something zapped painfully in her mind and the terminal points jabbed her. Another pain, this time going through her ankle and she knew exactly where she was, even before Veka opened her visor with one of those tight little half-smiles. Jily smiled back and tried to stand up. But the wall hit her shoulder and the floor came up to hit her face again.

Osip had wrapped her ankle tightly and Veka knelt, playing a sonic tube over it from the medical kit. Already the sound-waves, too high for the human ear, were relaxing the swollen muscle and Jily had three cups of coffee in her; she was feeling better.

They were in the sleeping quarters. Nel sat at the head of the table, her coffee untasted before her and her face as expressionless as the crook-tilt of her eyelid and lips allowed. Osip did most of the speaking and Nel's dark brown eyes went only once from his face to the dream-caps over each cubicle. She finally took a sip of coffee and grimaced. It was cold.

'No wonder they were all so twitchy when I came last time,' she said. 'You did well.'

And Jily knew Nel well enough to know that was a long speech of praise. Outside in the control chamber, the blue screen was still blank, but Nel's Copy sat at the consoles, continuously monitoring;

there was no communication with Earth yet, but the heavens round Venus seemed clear of Betels.

'I hope Angharad gets back to us soon,' said Veka.

Nel shrugged and muttered something about painted dummies. Without saying anything she had taken control in a very complete way, Jily sensed, as though she owned the base.

'I want a guided tour,' she said abruptly. Her solid face crook-frowned and she jerked a black-gloved thumb back at the row of dream-caps. 'In there.'

She's not surprised about anything, thought Jily. The Betels, the doomfire, even the explosives. Nel knew a hell of a lot more than she was telling. Those hard brown eyes were on her now.

'Just Jily and me.'

Jily didn't even have time to feel scared. Such was the authority in Nel's voice that she was already standing, just able to take the pain in her ankle, before two other voices spoke together.

'No.'

Veka and Osip had stood together, beside Jily. Nel's face twisted into a black scowl but they just looked back. Osip's arm slipped into hers.

'I just want Jily.' Nel's voice was like a laser drill.

'We told you about those deinos,' said Osip.

'I can handle them, kid.'

'We weren't thinking about you,' said Veka.

She slipped her arms into Jily's. Nel was still glaring, but they all just looked back and for the first time anywhere, Jily felt she *belonged*, she was part of other people. Nel stood up.

'All right, I'll programme my Copy for emergencies.' The crook-line of her mouth twisted a little. 'I'd be very interested to see your deinos.' She turned for the control room.

'Not if they see her first,' whispered Osip.

'I heard that, kid.' Nel didn't turn round and a moment later they heard her booted feet clumping over the control floor.

Jily was feeling a warm glow as though she'd swallowed another spoonful of doomfire. She looked up from Osip to Veka and all three grinned together. Jily tested her ankle again and decided Osip was right. It would take a very brave deino to bite Nel.

There was something wrong and bad – Jily sensed it the moment she zapped into the dreamstate. The trees and flowers were the same under the cloudy sky and it took a moment to realise there were no sounds of animals or birds. And not a sign of life anywhere – no swimming reptiles or fish in the river, no bat-winged pterodactyls overhead. There was no sign of the big dinosaurs and everywhere hung a frightened tense silence. Jily had felt that silence long ago, just before Kana and Dar told her about the crater explosion that made her an orphan.

'Where's everything gone?' said Osip.

Nel said nothing. She reached out quickly and took Jily's remote, then looked up and round at the low cloud cover and the quiet land. Then two things happened. A small purple and green dinosaur with a long pointed mouth and big eyes scuttled out of cover and ran in a blind zigzag, as though a night creature lost in the sunlight.

Nel swung round with a sharp look. Then a wind began to blow and the cloud cover seemed to swirl away; and they saw it, like a big, round, baleful ball of light in the heavens tinting everything blood-coloured round it. The red light beat on Nel's strong face.

'Is that it?' And for the first time, Jily saw fear in Nel's face.

'Yes,' shouted Osip. 'And bigger.'

'Hell fire sideways, kid, that's an asteroid on collision course – let's get out of here!'

Her hand went to the remote and suddenly there was an unearthly howling round them. A screaming melodic hum becoming more and more intense as though the very airwaves were bent and shrilling. Then the earth buckled at their feet and burst like a ripping seam between Nel and the kids. A jetting stream of white ice-light shot up and they jumped back. The seam gaped wider, dazzling a blinding blue-white and beating cold fire on their faces.

'Jump!' yelled Osip.

He grabbed Jily's hand and she grabbed Veka's as they leapt the gap. Jily crashed down, and the earth buckled again. She felt herself slipping back. In front of her, Nel was on her knees, a hand over her eyes. Jily looked up behind her.

'Nel – behind you!'

One of the giant trees was falling into the open, ice-bubbling crevasse. Nel rolled sideways as it crashed past her, the branches whipping Jily's face as it toppled into the boiling ice-light, turning white, freezing to every leaf tip as it sank from sight. Now Jily was slipping herself. She yelled again and Nel dived forward, a black-gloved hand closing on Jily's arm with the force of a door slamming. She pulled her back, yelling loud above the high screaming confusion.

'Kids!'

Veka and Osip were scrambling towards them. The screaming was louder and Jily rolled over to see the round ball of light filling the sky, pushing itself in slow motion through the layers of atmosphere and pulling them along like a stone ripping through curtains.

There were only seconds before it hit! The howling became a solid roar, the earth rippled and tore open and the ice-hot whiteness was flooding up. Then something clicked – she heard it clear and distinct in her ear and they were back in the sleeping quarters just as something jarred and seemed to shake them from top to toe. That meteor hitting, Jily thought – we were only just in time. Nel's face was whiter than Jily had ever seen it and she was slow getting off the bed. It takes a lot to shake her, Jily thought, but we managed it that time. They went into the living area and Nel sat heavily at the table.

'That blue-white stuff . . .?'

'Doomfire,' said Osip. 'Did you see what it did to that tree.'

'How did it suddenly appear like that?' Nel was even forgetting to be loud.

'Something from the planet,' said Jily. 'Coming out of the planet –' she hesitated. The stuff had jetted out like white blood. '– just before the asteroid struck.'

'*Because* the asteroid struck?' said Veka.

There was a little tremor round them and Nel took a deep breath. 'Veka, see if my Copy's got anything working yet.' She paused a moment longer, but Jily could see the old Nel take hold like a hand clenching into a fist. 'How far apart are they now?' she said abruptly.

'They . . .?' echoed Jily, puzzled.

'The tremors?' said Osip. Nel nodded. 'Every hour or so.'

'Forget them. Angharad said they're harmless.'

Nel was about to say something, the bitter, cynical twist back on her crook-lips when she looked back. 'Veka!' she yelled.

There was no answer. Nel crossed to the entrance in two long strides, Osip and Jily following. In the control area the motionless Copy still sat at the console, brass hands crossed tidily in its lap. Veka was there too, also silent and unmoving, her eyes going in their direction as they entered.

Beside her was a tall figure in a conical helmet with a single all-around eye slit. The heavy metal space suit had flared shoulders, ribbed arms and claw-gloves on the hands. It wore a long, shimmering tunic and had heavy iron feet. The claw gloves looked clumsy, but one of them held Veka firmly by the hand and the other pointed a strange device at them that looked unpleasantly like a gun.

'Do not move.' Jily had heard that patched sibilant voice before, just as she had heard those metal-clumping feet on the stairs of the mining chamber.

She was looking at a Betel.

The Betel put a claw-glove against Veka's back and gave her a hard push that sent her staggering over to tumble at Osip's feet. The gun-claw remained pointing steadily at them and the free claw went up to the metal eye-slitted head, knocking up a set of metal clips. Then it latched on to the side, half-twisted the helmet and with a very quick movement, threw if off. It clanged and rolled over the floor as

Veka scrambled to her feet. The thing pulled off a white hood and they looked into the face of the Betel alien.

Angharad.

18   Doomfire blazing

Another very tiny tremor ran through the base
and Jily felt her own insides tingle. Angharad, she
thought, but it's not. It had the same face but shorter
brown hair and a white small scar-line over one
eyebrow. There was a harder, more determined set
to the mouth and stained worker hands with chipped,
blunt fingernails.

'Betels.' Nel spoke in a flat, mocking voice.

'Call us what you like.' Her voice was harder than
Angharad's but with the same crystal tone. 'Anyone
who moves will end up very sizzled.'

'You're like Angharad,' whispered Veka.

'Even the best families fall out, don't they, Freya?'
said Nel with her twisted smile.

A second Betel was clanging up from the airlock
passage. One claw-glove was deftly unclipped and
the helmet pulled off – a man's face this time, a
light blue skin, long blue hair and blue eyes as
unwinking as a deino's. North–West Martian colony,
thought Jily. This is making sense and making new
questions. He stared at them without speaking, then
reached over the motionless Copy to press a console
button.

'Base secure.'

'Confirmed,' came a voice on the intercom.

Freya was still looking at Nel. These two know
each other, Jily thought. Then Freya gestured with

her gun, and they backed into the sleeping quarters. 'Get to work,' they heard her say to the man, and she kicked the door shut.

Nel went over to the table, her face expressionless as ever. 'They must have gone into holding on the other side of the planet, found their little firecracker didn't go off and come back – landed outside, through the ramp into my forward hatch then out the side exit into the airlock. Neat.' She pressed her hand down on a plastic coffee cup, crumpling it flat in tight suppressed anger.

'Who are they?' said Osip.

'Martian colonists,' said Nel with a sigh. 'They were keeping closer tabs than we thought.'

She looked round at the children. 'You see, Earth and the colonies have had a . . . disagreement.'

'The Martian colonies are in rebellion?' said Osip directly.

'Serious disagreement, that's all.' That bitter twist was back to Nel's lips again though. 'The Martians want more control over their mineral shipments.'

'So Earth wants a new energy source?' said Jily, and Nel nodded.

'Betels?' said Osip.

'No such things, kid.' Nel sighed again. 'A cover story to explain the disrupted shuttle service so nobody on Moonbase would get the same idea.'

'Why do the Martians want to stop Earth getting the doomfire?' said Veka.

'Power!' Nel slapped a black-gloved hand on a black-clad knee. 'A spoonful of that stuff powered Moonbase for a year, a block of it would power the Martian bases for – too long.'

'But there's tonnes of it there,' protested Veka.

'For the moment.' A little underfloor tremor underlined her words.

'Has finding that stuff made Venus unstable?' said Jily.

Nel looked at her. Even before she opened her mouth, Jily had the curious sense that Nel was telling her the direct truth. 'We don't know. Or even how that stuff works – it may be years before we do. Maybe just cutting it out will destabilise the whole mass.'

'Is that why you came back?' Again, that lock-to-lock sense between her and Nel. 'You were supposed to bring back more JOKS and you came early.'

'So did the Martians.' Those olive-green eyes held Jily for a moment, then looked away. That look away told Jily she was right, Nel *did* come back for them. Then Veka spoke and broke the closeness.

'The Martians will take us with them. They're humans—'

'They're Martian-humans and this is theft. This could start major retaliation.' Nel looked at them all. 'Hell fire sideways, they don't want witnesses.' She picked up the squashed coffee cup. 'They're getting more doomfire now, and all the solar system will be held to ransom by a bunch of grubby miners.' Nel's olive-green eyes looked round at the children and then at the brass-coloured hollow Copy head on the table. It rolled a little as a stronger tremor vibrated through the base. 'There is one way.' Now she was looking directly at Jily. 'My Copy is still out there.'

'I thought about that,' said Jily. 'They turned it off.'

'Then get inside and try to turn it on. You're our last chance.'

'Earth's last chance,' said Osip. 'Those Martians might take us.'

'Are you going to wait to find out?' Nel picked up the helmet in her black-gloved hands. 'I came back for you kids.'

'For us or the doomfire?' said Jily.

Nel crook-smiled and tossed the helmet to her like a basketball. 'Both. You owe me this.'

The last four words were directed at Jily alone. She remembered her terror and the strong hand that grabbed and pulled her away from the boiling silver-ice. Back in the Venus of pre-history, Nel had saved her life. The olive green eyes gleamed with a curious expression as Jily picked up the helmet. Triumph – or admiration?

'Jily—' said Osip.

Jily, you don't have to do this, he was going to say, but she abruptly shook her head, cutting him off. She slipped on the helmet and felt the hard contact points press against her head. Nel's face was back in that expressionless little crook-smile as Jily snapped the visor down and shut her eyes.

It was easier this time. There was a tiny buzz as somehow her mind boosted the circuits. Then that feeling of floating and a settling rigid closeness as her mind-awareness came alive inside the Copy. She could look through the visor at the console but not move anything. Near, through the open door, she could hear muffled voices and the hiss of a distant laser drill. The Martians were still at work.

The Copy was voice-activated to Nel, but there was a cut-off switch at the back. Jily sat there, imprisoned in the brass body-shell, and let the switch-image grow in her mind until it was clear and sharp as a hologram.

176

She could feel her awareness pulsing like bubbling water through the Copy circuits. She knew exactly what to do and the knowledge scared her a little. Now the image was super-sharp and she focused hard, turning the switch in her mind and feeling the switch at the back of her head turn as well. Straight away her Copy hands relaxed their stiff pose and she told her Copy body to stand.

Copies could move very silently, something that Jily knew all too well. This one would have to be super-quiet because both those Martians were armed. She walked to the open door and paused. The chamber below was empty, those muffled voices coming from the tunnel. She heard the man grumbling. 'We don't need another piece.'

'Too good a chance to miss,' came Freya's voice and there was the squeak of a trolley wheel. They were coming back.

Jily ran lightly down the stairs, so lightly she almost wanted to spring into the air and hover. Freya and the man came into view, pulling the trolley between them, their heads down. Jily grinned, as much as it was possible for her mind to grin, and stepped lightly in front of them. She tensed with incredible power as Freya looked up and saw her.

Her reactions were as fast as Nel's, her hand already reaching for the gun as Jily's Copy arm flashed out and wrenched it clear, crushing the barrel in her steel grip.

'Shouldn't be greedy,' she heard her Copy voice say. The man was slower to react and Jily waited till his gun was out before she kicked hard, slamming it up into the ice-ceiling. Then she stepped forward, much faster than human speed, grabbed their heads

and banged them together. Jily had always wanted to
do that to an adult. The two collapsed in a heap over
the trolley, groaning and stunned.

Jily picked up the man's gun. 'They won't be
moving for a few minutes,' she muttered to herself
and ran back upstairs. The key was in the lock of the
sleeping quarters door but she couldn't resist kicking
it open. It was something else she'd always wanted to
do and the startled look on Nel's face was worth it.

Nel did a very complete job of tying up the two
Martians; although they were still only half-conscious
and not even muttering, she gagged them as well.
Then she did something even more puzzling. She
wrenched the head off every Copy in the base and
sent them up the rubbish cute. She's making sure I
don't get back into those Copies, Jily thought, and
a little alarm began to tingle away in her mind.
Then, blending in, a loud sonic hum came from
the console screen and Nel showed her strong white
teeth in a grin.

'Corp.'

The blue screen gloss-shimmered into life. Angharad
and Herilbert were there, standing with an empty
chair between them. Both were relaxed, their faces
carefully smooth but – but they're not looking at
us, thought Jily. The sonic hum faded, but that
little alarm was tingling more quickly in her mind
as Gobnait appeared and took her place in the chair,
sitting motionless as Nel gave her report. Gobnait
didn't look at them either.

'Very good,' she said, her face closed of emotion. The strong pink hands came tightly together
and the image enhancing eyes looked at Jily, Osip

and Veka for the first time. 'Children, Corp is grateful.'

The bland, dismissive way she spoke those words made Jily chill. They said, you are nothing, less than nothing, you have fulfilled your duty to Corp.

'And we are looking forward to Earth,' said Veka with a happy grin, waiting to be complimented.

'Earth.' Angharad's voice was as sweet and crystal as ever. 'All this must remain secret. You cannot come to Earth.'

'What?' whispered Veka, white-faced and stunned.

'You will be assigned duties on Spoke.'

'You promised us *Earth*!' shouted Osip.

'No!' Angharad's voice rang with crystal steel. 'I said *Earth*-children belonged on Earth. You.' She was looking at Osip. Beside her, Gobnait's pink hands came apart again.

'There are quite enough people on Earth without Moon clones adding to our number.' Herilbert that time and beside him, Gobnait raised a pink hand as though pulling a vocal string. 'Besides, Jily will need . . . special examination because of her powers.'

What was it Veka had said once, thought Jily, Corp doesn't muck around. No, and right now Corp is ripping the dream-cover reality, telling us in cutting surgical words just how unimportant we really are. And me, I'm going to stay a white rat in a cage—

'I won't go to Earth,' said Osip. 'Not without the others.'

'You'll do as you are told,' said Gobnait. Her voice was sharp, stung, as though Osip had really offended her. 'You are part of the elite—'

'No!' shouted Osip.

'Yes!' flashed Gobnait, but Osip just glared into the laser blast of her words.

'Nel.' Angharad interrupted smoothly. 'Shut down – and keep your JOKs in order.'

'Your JOKS!' Jily heard herself shout but the screen flickered and went glossy-blank.

'Yes.' Nel turned, the crook-smile in place and one hand casually on the black handle of her gun. 'Be good little JOKS and you'll come out smiling.'

'What's happening?' whispered Veka, still looking at the blank screen as though she'd been slapped.

'Power. Corp dominating, winner taking all.' The flat bitter amusement in Nel's voice dismissed all human emotions and her eyes went to Jily like olive-green stones. 'In this case, Corp and Parthenope.'

The same expression was back in her eyes that Jily saw when she put on the Copy helmet in the sleeping quarters. Not admiration but triumph. She was sick now at thinking how she had helped this woman because, too late, it was all too clear. The last little piece of mystery was slotting into place even as Osip spoke.

'Parthenope is under the rock-fall.'

'No.' Jily felt tired and sick. '*She's* Parthenope.'

Nel's crook-smile became a twisted grin of victory.

'When the first three had their accident, I wanted three more. One who knew about early life-forms, one for botany, and one . . .' The olive-green eyes looked at Jily again. '. . . who had strong mindspread.'

'Why just JOKS?' said Veka bitterly as her laser flared. Her red hair hung in a straggly mop over her shoulders.

'Easy to control.' The crook-smile stayed in place. Jily couldn't think of her as Parthenope – she was Nel, the senior shuttle pilot who chanced on an incredible Venusian secret in time to save Earth from Martian blackmail. And who had brought them back down the ice-tunnel for a last solid chunk of doomfire.

'What are Moon clones?' said Jily.

'Yes, I want to know that too.'

Veka defiantly cut her laser and looked down the tunnel to where Nel stood, gun in hand, the bound and gagged North Martians propped up against the far wall behind her. Osip just looked from one to the other, the closed set look on his face.

'Later.' Nel scowled and made a jabbing movement with her gun.

'You're like Martians, cloned from gene cells, not born.' Freya had managed to work her gag loose and spoke quickly. 'Gene kids are just numbers and a bar code to Corp and the World Council.' Nel's gun swung in her direction, but she ignored it. 'Earth has genetically designed you for life in outer space. You have brown skins, Erl here has a blue one. He was tinted so he could never go to Earth and live a normal life.'

'Martian skin colours are part of the protection against solar radiation or something,' said Nel. 'Freya is a malcontent from Earth, a loser. You are all normal – now get on with it!'

'Normal?' Freya winced as Nel's boot thudded in her ribs. 'Look at your hands, kids!'

'Keep working!' screamed Nel.

Jily and Veka weren't listening. Both looked at their hands, cold and tingling, somehow supercharged with the frozen energy force they had been holding. In the centre of their palms was a small code and number sequence. JLY 10–02, Jily Tennoto, she read and looked at Veka's. VKA B4, Veka Beafor. This time it was the blue-skinned Erl who spoke, his voice hard with a tight hatred.

'Those numbers weren't supposed to appear on your hands for a year or two yet. The doomfire made them appear somehow.' His angry look dared Nel to kick him as well. 'Gene kids, Corp property with no human rights, unless—'

'Unless you come with us to Mars,' finished Freya.

'Shut up!' Nel's eyes were like olive-green stones. 'Numbers or names, keep working.'

'Yes, keep working,' said Osip and all at once, he sounded like a superior Earth-person.

'Oh sure, Earth kid!' Veka spat the words like an insult, but her laser flared into bitter life again.

Osip was looking at Jily, then quickly upward. She started her own laser torch into the ice-face and another small tremor ran through as she did. Then she let herself glance casually up as she wiped some sweat from her forehead. Overhead ran the long dark tendrils of tiger-weed trapped frozen in the silver-ice.

'You've got your grades and Corp won't forget you.' Nel sounded as though she actually wanted them to believe it.

'Corp can get—' Veka's last word was muttered under the vicious hiss of her laser. Jily nudged her.

'Keep in a straight line, keep up,' she said.

Veka glanced up, the sweat-lines running down her face. Then she nodded, registering very quickly. The laser swung in her hand, still flaring, straight into the ice-ceiling. Around them, huge silvery blue drops of melted doomfire splashed down.

'Hurry,' said Nel coldly.

'Sorry, boss,' said Veka meekly. 'Corp-clone B-4 is doing its best.' Her laser swung up again and the heat-line travelled across the ceiling. Silver drops splattered down the tunnel and one splashed on Nel's black shoulder like bright silver metal.

Jily was feeling the power of doomfire more strongly than she ever had; so she made it thought-project down the flare of her laser. *Go* doomfire, she thought, down into the heat-line of my laser and form over Nel's head. She swung her own torch up for a moment and Veka looked at her. The girl's frantic energy had gone. But when Jily looked up again, the ice was melting in a long groove, and over Nel's head a shallow saucer depression had opened, a knot of the tiger-weed showing clearly through. Then the chunk of doomfire cracked and jolted itself outward. 'Get it on the trolley.' Nel's voice was uneasy now and another little tremor went through the tunnel. The alot tubes stacked to one side tinkled together a little and Nel's voice snapped with a vicious edge. 'Move!'

Osip helped them load the chunk onto the trolley and pull it up the steps from the alcove. Jily looked up again. Over Nel, the weed-knot was free of the ice, untangling itself, snaking down long tendrils to Nel's booted feet.

'What about them?' asked Jily, indicating Freya and Erl.

'I may leave them here.' Nel kept her eyes and gun firmly on the children. 'They set the explosives, they can live with them.'

'Sounds right to me,' said Osip with a secret evil smile.

It was too much. Nel's suspicions were instantly aroused, but even as she glared round, the tiger-weed circled and looped tight round her ankle. Another loop snatched round her gun hand and Veka pushed the trolley forward. It crashed into Nel's legs and she fell heavily, tiger-weed wrapping round her.

'Come on!' shouted Osip and the tunnel tremored again as he spoke. Jily shot a look at the tinkling alot tubes and ran.

More of the tiger-weed was breaking clear, curling down. They ducked it and ran into the mining chamber, pulling the traps from Freya and the man. The tunnel tremored again.

'All this movement will destabilise that alot,' shouted Freya. 'Run!' Erl was still dazed and she grabbed his hand, pulling him to the stair. Osip and Veka were already following, but Jily looked back. Nel was looped and entwined in the red and green tendrils, kicking hard but trapped. With a sick feeling, Jily saw a tendril wrap round the woman's neck; she snatched up the laser drill and headed back.

'Jily!' shouted Osip.

She swept it round and tendrils fell, severed. This doesn't make sense, she thought, but she could feel Nel's hand pulling her out of that boiling ice chasm.

Tiger-weed tendrils sprang at her like evil fingers, then another was chopped as it touched her face. Veka was beside her, laser drill flaring.

'You're mad!' shouted Veka, as Jily pulled Nel clear of the wrapping, tangling weeds. The tunnel shook and ice chunks crashed down as a huge knot of the red and green weed fell free and began untangling.

'Let's get out of here!' shouted Osip. They backed down the passage and up the stairs. The weed exploded after them in a writhing snake-like tangle, already braiding itself into a strong, thick mass.

Osip slammed the door and they were back in the control room. 'Kids, come on!' shouted Freya from the tunnel. Then suddenly on-screen Angharad appeared – a different Angharad, her hair tousled as though she'd been pulling it, even her make-up smeared.

'Children – Osip – come to Earth. We need you!'

'No!' shouted Osip.

'You are my son!' Her voice began to gabble as though a sound-track was speeding up. 'Had to prove you, come back to Earth, bring other children, doomfire, promise we'll—'

'No!' shouted Osip again.

Angharad's voice had cut and her face suddenly filled the screen, so huge that they could have run into her open mouth; then the screen distorted, dragging her mouth down in a sagging dismay before flicking to blankness. Osip was still standing there, his face white. Jily grabbed him and pointed frantically at the control monitors.

'Look!'

In the ice-tunnel, the tiger-weed had grown like a huge lashing snake-monster and already the door was thudding under repeated blows. Freya yelled again and, holding Nel's arms and legs, the three kids ran down the corridor, throwing her bodily through the airlock.

'Do you know the systems on this shuttle?' gasped Freya.

'Yes,' said Jily.

And after watching Nel so long, she did – almost. She threw herself into the control chair. 'Emergency take-off!' she shouted. It was a gamble but Nel would have her shuttle ready. The lights glowed, the zap-zap voice answered and the shuttle began gathering power. Above them, the entry lock was opening into the red glare of Venus, but Jily was watching a nightmare on the flight deck vision monitors.

They were still linked to the base. Inside, the tiger-weed, now knotted into monster thickness, had broken down the door and was coiling along the passage to the airlock. And below, the ice-tunnel was shaking, big chunks falling as more weed escaped.

'Hell!' screamed Freya beside her.

She saw what Jily had done. Now the weed below was among the jiggling alot sticks, waving and looping, tightening to crush and break them. The detonator triggers flashed evil, green, death eyes at the screen and Freya forced herself to speak calmly.

'Can we get off before that lot blows?'

'Maybe.'

But with a queer cold certainty, Jily knew they couldn't. The shuttle was moving, but on-screen the tiger-weed was crushing and snapping the alot sticks.

186

The green death eyes flared and the monitor screen fuse-flashed as the shuttle gathered speed. Too late!

Jily shut her eyes as Purple Zero exploded round them.

19   Doomfire on Venus

It was the base layout that saved their lives, and the alot sticks scattering before they exploded. The force of the explosion punched itself down the ice-tunnel, up the stairs and across the control area. As the shuttle began moving, the explosion force gathered behind, slamming them up out of the entry tunnel, the shockwaves spreading themselves out into the red storming hell of Venus itself. On either side, the whole base was opening in a huge burst, knocking them even further up into the orange storm mass.

'Trim flight!' screamed Freya, but Jily's hands were already flickering over the controls as though encased in Nel's black gloves. All those hours under a virtual reality helmet paid off as the shuttle wobbled, steadied, and she took it in a steep climb. Another shockwave hit them from below and Jily glanced down. The explosion seemed to be hopping crazily across the red surface. It's started, she thought. We've set off the doomfire and the reaction may blow Venus apart because we trespassed – and we're still too close. Then the cloud-cover closed round them and Jily welcomed the acid-laden thickness because even shockwaves could not penetrate this solid blanket. But they had to get out quickly – as soon as they could!

'I think we're safe now,' came Freya's voice and Jily looked back. The woman smiled, a big relieved grin and Jily relaxed, because anybody who smiled like that had to be all right.

'What was that crazy spaceship?' said Osip.

'Just a souped-up old donkey.' She stopped grinning. 'Kids, we thought Purple Zero was empty when we set that alot stuff.'

'We hid in the Copy suits.' Veka grinned. 'Jily's idea.'

Freya grinned back. 'Sorry about sending those Copies mad. We were trying wavelengths and must have sent a power surge through them.'

'We never did like Copies.'

Freya laughed. 'You kids will do well on Mars.' Then all three of them looked at Osip, over by the wall. 'Osip, we can send you back to Earth—'

'No.'

He shook his head. Jily knew he was thinking about the mother who ignored him until it suited her plans. And if Earth-people were like that, then Osip was better on Mars.

'When the multi-nationals on Earth knew it was time to mine the solar resources, they didn't have any options. Earth's population was down to five per cent after the plagues and pollution, so they cloned a new breed for outer space.' Freya paused and looked at Erl and he looked back, his blue eyes still unwinking. 'Genetically engineered so their bodies would stand the different demands and pressures. And genetically tinted, blue and green for Mars and red for the Asteroids. No health reasons. Just so they could never return to Earth.'

'Without sticking out like freaks,' said Erl softly.

'But we're not those colours,' said Veka to Freya.

'Moonbase kids are in-between,' she explained,

then added with a sigh, 'and some of us on Earth didn't want this. So we were shunted out to the solar colonies to make our own settlement in the south, away from the blue, green and red people. Earth used colour to keep us apart.' She gave a sad little smile. 'Not for the first time in history.'

'But Mars was a different planet,' said Erl and a small, thin smile curved on his lips. 'And we are different people.'

Shockwaves were bumping up through the clouds, but they were nearly at the upper atmosphere now.

'Will Earth let you be different?' asked Veka.

Freya gave a weary sigh. 'Maybe—'

She grunted and fell forward. Nel was standing there, blood still trickling down one side of her face, pointing a short black stun-rod at them.

'We're going to Earth.'

Foolish, *foolish* to have left her alone, apparently unconscious. The twisted anger in her face made her more crook-mouthed than ever. Below, more shockwaves were thumping through the cloud-cover and Jily wondered how long before the planet itself exploded. Osip moved and the black rod swung in his direction.

'These things drop a Copy by fusing its circuits. I hate to think what they'd do to the human brain.'

'There's room on Mars for all of us,' said Jily.

'Earth.' Nel crook-smiled again. 'Corp and Senior Vice-President in charge of pension funds will suit me fine.' The stun-rod kept turning, covering them all. 'Now stand back from the controls, Jily.'

Jily stayed where she was. 'Don't you mean JLY 10–02?'

Something like an electric sledge-hammer was

191

smashing into her hand. Jily yelled and Nel's crook-smile stayed in place as she lowered the black tube. Below and round them, the cloud-cover was rippling as though something was breaking through.

'No choices, kid,' said Nel.

'We saved your life!' shouted Veka.

'And I will save yours,' said Nel implacably. 'But only to the count of three.' She said the words with a deliberate emphasis. 'One.'

Jily's hand felt like a door had slammed on it. She didn't move and neither did Veka or Osip. Below now, the shockwaves were pounding up against the shuttle and red light was glinting through the orange cloud mass.

'Two.' She half-shook her head, saying more plainly than words, you stupid kids, I am serious.

'You can't fly this shuttle to Earth on your own,' Jily heard Osip say, but she had shut her eyes. Mindspread: she had bounced again, thumped and shaken into electronic blackness. When she opened her eyes again she was looking at herself. At the black-haired girl in the blue track suit standing by the controls, scared but defiant. She could feel a dark iron closeness around her, she could feel her hand holding back the black rod; she could sense the frustration, the anger, the desperation. She was looking through olive-green eyes at the black-haired girl who spoke as though in a dream.

'Nel, you don't want to kill us,' she screamed and an angry black hail-storm raged round her; it screamed of the long, lonely, endless hours of space flight, growing old in the service of Corp, danger, unrewarded courage, hail-storming in Nel's howling tones. But her Jily-hand was on the stun-rod and her Jily-voice said, sharp and silver in the darkness, 'No, Nel, you can't kill us.' Then sideways, she saw Freya's boot come out, kick Nel's legs from underneath; she felt Nel stagger, she saw the black haired Jily jump back, flipping down the control column. Then everything became a crazy jostling chaos as the shuttle stood on its head and dived back into the orange cloud.

And with zap-click speed she was back in herself and pulling the control stick back. Freya, Veka and Nel were in a tangled heap, Osip was diving into it. The whole mass crashed forward as the dive steepened, Veka's foot came out and kicked the stun-rod under the control seat.

Jily was trying to pull the stick back as the heavy thick cloud swirled past. Red streaks like forked lightning cut past and the shuttle thudded and jarred from end to end. Just as Jily regained control, the last cloud strip fled past. And a solid stomach bounce told Jily more clearly than words what was happening below.

Where Purple Zero had been, a solid column of blue-gold doomfire was spouting into the air. Around it, the red-baked surface split and cracked like a pie-crust in all directions; then a stronger burst punched up into the cloud layer overhead, like a gold-blue fist smashing into a wall. Venus *won't* explode, said the bounce in Jily's stomach. The body-heap beside her was untangling itself. Nel was securely grabbed by three pairs of hands, but all Jily could do was watch that terrible scene below – as Venus came *alive*.

The gold-blue doomfire column was higher now and the shuttle whirled round it like a dead leaf round a giant storm-lashed tree. The cloud thickness was rolling back and through it came a dazzling shaft of sunlight, fusing with the doomfire like two sharp spears. Below, the red land cracked more widely open, glinting bubbling streams of blue-gold everywhere as the life-force of Venus spilled through.

Airblasts kicked under the shuttle like a mad carpet and the force threw Jily against the control stick as she struggled to hold the craft steady. That cloud cover, four kilometres thick, was swirling away as sunlight and doomfire grew together in intensity. Then the blue-gold arched away in huge waterfall droplets over the deep ravine around Aphrodite Terra. Most sunlight streamed through the torn clouds and as the doomfire fell back, new clouds of steam arose.

Nel had been tied up and Freya dragged her into the cargo hold. Osip and Veka stood behind the control chair, looking down as the steam-clouds rose, split with dazzling arrow-shafts of blue-gold. They were mixing into a sharp stabbing green, the colour of life; new clouds were forming and tears came to Jily's eyes as she realised what was happening.

For the first time in two hundred million years, life was returning to Venus.

Once, a long time ago, Earth and Venus were twin planets – far enough away to be in balance and close enough to evolve together with the same life-forms. Then a giant asteroid or moon had come crashing into their skies like a runaway truck with the brakes off. Both planets were in the age of the dinosaurs. Venus was directly hit and knocked sideways, spinning out of orbit. The same force ended the dinosaur age on

Earth and the asteroid was caught by Earth's gravity, becoming the Moon.

'But all living planets have their own life-force,' Jily said. 'When Venus was knocked spinning, I think it went into emergency shutdown . . . like . . . like a swimmer taking a deep breath before being pulled under deep water. Venus froze the air in its lungs.'

Then when it stopped spinning and settled in orbit, a cloud cover kept the sunlight out. There was no life-making solar energy. And the gravity became too strong, the cloud cover packed in the heat—

'And below, the energy became too solid to let Venus come back to life.' Jily spoke as though all the doomfire was flooding through her body; she saw it more sharply and real than a dream-cap hologram. Through her words, she could see Venus tumbling on its doomride across the solar system to the orbit of today.

'Venus held its breath? The heat was packed under the cloud-cover, the doomfire held underground—' Veka stopped, struggling to understand.

'Totally opposing forces locking together like checkmate. Extremes of heat and cold keeping each other together.' Osip looked at Jily. 'And apart.'

'Yes.'

Freya was back and gently nudged Jily out of the control chair. The shuttle was tilting upward again. 'We should raise a signal for our link-ship soon,' said Freya.

'Then?' said Osip.

'Long, strong talks with Earth.' Freya smiled again. 'Jily, with your powers, you'll have to be on the negotiating team.'

'If they last.' Jily hadn't told anyone about getting

into Nel's mind and, anyway, didn't know how long her powers would last away from Venus. She felt unreal and trembly and her hand hurt.

'Go and rest,' said Veka with a sympathetic grin. Jily nodded and as she went out into the cargo hold, she heard Veka say to Freya, 'Hey, what are South Marshie guys like?' and Freya's reply, 'Veka, they won't know what hit them.'

In the cargo hold, Erl, was sitting up, rubbing his head. Jily gave him some water and went over to the cabin. Nel was inside, strapped to a chair. Jily shut the door.

'You thought you were using us, Nel. But Corp was using us all.'

'You should have left me in the tiger-weed.' Nel's eyes were olive-green stones.

'Everything will change now.'

'I stopped changing years ago, kid.'

Nel didn't know that Jily had stood inside her soul – that she had sensed black iron darkness, but no evil. Just the dark, cold, unhappy iron. There would be time on the flight to talk to Nel and understand her.

'Well, you can change.' Jily got up to go. 'I know it.' And because she knew it, she gave a big happy smile. Nel twisted angrily, uncomfortably, in her chair.

'What's so bloody amusing, JOK?'

'I'll tell you on Mars.'

She shut the door on the scowling, defiant, black-clad woman. Jily was still smiling. It would be a hard fight, but she knew she would win. Outside, through the porthole, a twinkling light was approaching; the Martian link-ship coming alongside.

Behind it was the huge, shining, yellow glove of Venus. On Earth, Gobnait, Angharad and the others would see that new golden signal in black space and know that things had changed forever in the solar system. Jily turned as a hand touched her shoulder.

'Nothing'll be the same,' said Osip.

'Nothing has to be, Osip.'

She put out her hand and Osip took it. His smile was a little less certain than hers and they kissed. Osip would still need her strength and Jily was happy to give it. And she was happy thinking about Nel because that was a battle she intended to win before the shuttle docked at Mars. Even if it would be tough – tougher than teaching those deinos how to hologram-paint their claws. Jily laughed at the thought and kept on laughing. Osip looked at her, puzzled.

'What's so funny?'

Jily decided to kiss him again. 'I'll tell you on Mars,' she said.

THE GHOSTS OF TRITON

Ken Catran

Dex must clear his name. A routine mining exploration has ended in tragedy – and Dex has been blamed. But who will believe him?

The answer lies on Triton, millions of kilometres away. First Dex must overcome the hatred of the shuttle crew that takes him there. Then he must face an alien puzzle too terrifying to imagine.

THE SHADOW OF PHOBOS

Ken Catran

Cela, a Martian colonist, is kidnapped and taken to Earth. Telesforo, an Earth-boy on an urgent mission, crash-lands on Mars. Now, both teenagers are being stalked by an unknown killer.

One thing links them. Something that will wake horrors long since forgotten. Something that will change the solar system for ever.